angel's choice

angel's choice

LAUREN BARATZ-LOGSTED

SIMON PULSE

New York London Toronto Sydney

SIMON PULSE
An imprint of Simon & Schuster Children's Publishing Division
1230 Avenue of the Americas, New York, NY 10020
Copyright © 2006 by Lauren Baratz-Logsted
All rights reserved, including the right of reproduction
in whole or in part in any form.
SIMON PULSE and colophon are registered trademarks of
Simon & Schuster, Inc.
Designed by Karin Paprocki
The text of this book was set in Cochin.
Manufactured in the United States of America
First Simon Pulse edition December 2006
2 4 6 8 10 9 7 5 3 1
Library of Congress Control Number 2005938021
ISBN-13: 978-1-4169-2524-8
ISBN-10: 1-4169-2524-4

For all the girls who have been there,
and for all the different choices they have made;
and for Nicole Baratz and Caroline Logsted,
nieces extraordinaire

ACKNOWLEDGMENTS

THANK YOU TO MY AGENT PAMELA HARTY FOR BEING SO good to me, and thank you to all the other wonderful people at The Deidre Knight Agency.

Thank you to my editor Julia Richardson for being a sheer pleasure to work with and for making my dream a reality; and thank you to her assistant Siobhan Wallace and the rest of the terrific Simon & Schuster team. I'd be remiss if I didn't also thank sister authors Anne Ursu and Gretchen Laskas for introducing me to the marvelous Julia.

Special thanks to Sue Estabrook and Nicki Thomas for always helping me make my work better than it would be otherwise.

Thank you to my family and friends, in particular my mother Lucille Baratz, for sustaining me with love and laughter.

As always, it's impossible to thank my husband Greg Logsted and our daughter Jackie enough for everything they are, for the better person they inspire me to be.

august

6:00 p.m.

SCHOOL WILL START UP AGAIN NEXT WEEK, AND I AM AT
Ricky D'Amico's end-of-summer blowout. I do not
think I was number one on her list of people to invite —
I was probably not even number fifty-one — but her
next-door neighbor is my best friend, Karin, and she
couldn't very well not invite her next-door neighbor,
and once she invited Karin, Karin asked me to stop by.

Ricky D'Amico has never liked me. First week of
freshman art class, nearly three years ago now, she
thought I purposefully said something to insult her — I
didn't; it was just a stupid joke — and she has never forgiven me.

By the time I arrive, walking there from my house
two blocks away, it looks like the other fifty people who
were on the guest list ahead of me are already there.
Many of the guys and some of the girls are clustered

1

around the keg just outside the garage. Ricky D'Amico has the kind of cool parents who say it's okay for us kids to drink, even though we're all underage, so long as no one drives and they don't get busted for giving alcohol to minors. They say so long as we are responsible, there's no harm in having a little fun.

It's only six o'clock, so it'll be light out for nearly another three hours, and when I look over by the pool area, the late-afternoon summer sun still fairly high in the sky, I see most of the girls hanging around there, red plastic cups of beer in their hands. But none of them are swimming. The D'Amicos have one other rule: no swimming while drinking.

A couple of kids yell out "Hey!" to me, but no one approaches, leaving it instead for me to decide where I'll go first. I used to think maybe this kind of thing meant people didn't like me—well, okay, Ricky D'Amico doesn't—but lately I think it is because most people are so scared of being rejected. They're scared that if they act all happy to see you, and come running over like a puppy dog, you'll be looking over their shoulder trying to find someone better.

I look at both groups of kids—the one by the keg,

the one by the pool—trying to decide where to go first. I recognize all of the girls, of course: Sherry Bixby, the junior varsity head cheerleader; Dawn Peck, who everyone thinks will be a great artist someday and who always wears these romantic gauzy clothes she designs herself; Kirstin Thomas, who is so smart that it scares boys, but who is also so pretty and perky, no one ever leaves her out of anything; and all the other JV cheerleaders, artists, and pretty girls. I size up what they are wearing and decide that I have not done too bad for myself tonight: While I'll never dress as cool as Kirstin and her crowd, my jeans fit well, with no bulges hanging over the side; my white gauze shirt is acceptable without being arty; even my makeup is right for once, making me look like I care about what I look like, but not too much, while highlighting my dark eyes. I am particularly happy that, despite it being August, there is little humidity, so my long dark hair is not turning into the finger-in-the-light-socket look it's capable of developing. At least not yet. My heeled sandals make me four inches taller than my usual tiny height, and I am not falling over in them yet, two things that always make me ridiculously happy. And my smile is good — God knows, my parents paid enough for it.

But even though I feel as though I look good enough to approach the girls at the pool, when I look closer, I realize Karin isn't there. And when you go to a party where the hostess doesn't really want you there, it's always best to locate your best friend first.

So I turn my attention to the kids gathered around the keg, and I do not see Karin there, either, but as I draw closer, making my way through the crowd, I do see something that is maybe even better: Danny Stanton is seated in a lawn chair next to the keg, taking it upon himself to keep everyone's red plastic cups filled.

I have been in love with Danny Stanton it seems like, sometimes, forever.

"Hey! Angel!" Danny says, obviously happy to see me. He reaches for another red plastic cup. "Let me get you a brewski."

Angel really is my name, Angel Hansen. My mother, who is only forty-two, loved a book called *That Was Then, This Is Now* by S. E. Hinton when she was a preteen. Even though the girl nicknamed Angel in the book isn't very nice, Mom loved the name and made sure it went down on my birth certificate as Angel, so that no one could ever call me Angela or Angie by mistake.

"Hey, Danny," I say, keeping my voice even, not wanting to sound too excited to see him, even though I am.

When I say it seems like I have been in love with Danny Stanton forever, it is no exaggeration. Toward the end of freshman year Danny asked me out. Danny is very tall with black hair, and brown eyes that are even more beautiful than chocolate. I was so surprised when he asked me out—it wasn't like we traveled in the same circles exactly—but he seemed to think I was funny in a good way, and he laughed at all my jokes. We first talked to each other on a Wednesday in mid-June, skipping both our classes for the rest of the day and hanging out in the cafeteria until it was time to go home, when he walked me to my bus. On Friday he had me go over to his house, and while I loved it when he kissed me, I was relieved when he didn't try for more. On Saturday he had his father drop us off at the movies and we did a little more than kiss, but not much. On Sunday we were supposed to go out again, but then he called to say he'd decided to get back together with his old girl-friend, one of the freshman cheerleaders. I didn't know what I'd done wrong. We'd had a good time together—you can't miss it when the other person is having a good time—and I even made the mistake of crying a little bit on the phone and getting bitchy a little bit when he said he was going back with his old girlfriend; I was that hurt.

I hadn't even known he had an old girlfriend.

Now, two years later, I am still hoping for a second chance.

When he said two years ago that he was going back to his old girlfriend, even though I was hurt, I totally understood it. After all, why would someone like Danny Stanton want to go out with someone like me? He was gorgeous, everyone knew he was going to be a great basketball player, he was the most popular boy in school. Even the people who *hated* jocks *liked* Danny Stanton. And what was I? I was the unremarkable girl, the girl who wasn't awful but certainly wasn't great, the girl who could sometimes crack a decent joke but who mostly just disappeared into the woodwork.

And still I am hoping for that second chance, because Danny Stanton has never stopped being nice to me, not once, not even when I got all teary and bitchy on the phone with him that one time. Two years later he still acts as though I'm someone sort of special. I know this because, even though he has gone through many girlfriends since that cheerleader freshman year, when we run into each other at parties, he always hooks up with me if whatever girlfriend he is going out with at the time isn't around. We don't have sex—I've never had sex—but we do a lot of other things. He doesn't do this with anyone else.

Karin sometimes says that he uses me, but I don't believe this. He could have anyone he wants, he could certainly have more variety in his life, so why does he keep coming back to me?

"Maybe it's because he's always drunk when he sees you," Karin said one time.

This may sound like a mean thing to say, like she's saying he *only* would want me if he were drunk. But Karin is my best friend and I know she is just trying to protect me.

Just to prove it to her, though, I had her drive me to his house one time last year before I had my own license. It was only two in the afternoon, so I figured he had to be sober.

"I'll bet I can get him to kiss me inside of five minutes," I told her.

"And that'll *prove* something?" she said.

"Okay, maybe it won't *prove* anything," I admitted, "but it'll feel good."

And he did kiss me, sober, and it did feel good.

For two years now, I have been telling myself that if I can just get Danny Stanton in the right moment, he will see that the reason he asked me out in the first place two years ago, the reason he keeps coming back to me again time after time after time, is because he is as much in love with me as I am with him.

Now as I look down at him sitting in that lawn chair, that sweet, goofy grin on his face, I smile back. "Sure. Pull me a beer."

I start to drink.

7:00 p.m.

Karin finally finds me where I am still standing by the keg, next to Danny Stanton.

"Hey!" Karin gives me a big hug, the kind of strong full-body hug best friends give each other, sometimes

8

even if they just saw each other yesterday, like it is that good to have the other person in the world.

I hug her back, hard, so glad she is my best friend. In the process I spill some of my beer on both of us.

"Sorry," I say, pulling away.

Karin laughs.

"Who cares?" she says.

I see Ricky D'Amico walk up to the other side of Danny Stanton where he is still seated in his lawn chair, pulling beers for people, her auburn hair startling over a lime green halter top, her legs long in a pair of microshorts that are maybe a total of three inches in length from well below her navel to her crotch, and I think, *Ricky D'Amico would care if I spilled a beer on her.*

Karin laughs again, reminding me why she is my best friend when she adds, "I'll only spill some on myself eventually anyway. Thanks for saving me the trouble."

Even though Karin is prettier than I am, with short dark-blond hair streaked with gold and honey, in a boyish cut that somehow makes her look even prettier, blue eyes like the best of the blue paints in art class, a figure she doesn't have to worry about, and a sense of style that is original without looking forced; even though she is smarter than I am, a sure thing for Yale where I'm only an if; even though she is more popular than I am and even Ricky D'Amico kind of likes her . . . none of that matters. She is my best friend because she always makes me feel as though she has always liked me, will always like me, for me. She never makes me feel *less than* in any way.

Karin takes a beer from Danny Stanton, then she grabs on to my hand, tugs me toward the pool area.

"Come on," she says, "let's go where the action is."

But I perform what Mr. Davis in physics class would call an equal and opposite reaction to her action: I resist.

"What?" she says.

"I just think I'll stay here for a bit," I say.

"Why?" she says.

My back is to Danny Stanton, meaning he can't see my face when I give my chin a little move upward, raising my eyebrows a bit, like I'm trying to say, "Behind me."

"What?" Karin says again, confused.

Frustrated, I mouth the two words that are pretty much the most precious to me in the world: "Danny Stanton."

Now it's Karin's turn to be frustrated.

"Aren't you ever going to give that up?" she says.

"No," I say, "not ever."

"Well," she says, dropping my hand, "when you come to your senses, I'll be over by the pool."

I turn back toward the keg and am surprised to see Danny sitting there alone now.

"Hey," he says to me again, more quietly than before, as though he's just seeing me tonight for the first time. "It's Angel Hansen."

"That's me," I say, feeling kind of dumb even as I say it, but then realizing it doesn't matter how dumb I sound because from the looks of Danny's lazy smile he's already well on the way to being pretty drunk.

Danny reaches out suddenly, grabbing on to the same hand Karin tugged on just a few minutes ago. He studies my hand like it's the most interesting thing in the world, rubbing my fingers with his thumb. Then he puts his beer down next to the lawn chair and squints up at me, shading his eyes with the same hand that was just holding the beer. "You know what I like best about you, Angel Hansen?" he says.

I'm so surprised by his words, by the important sound of his words, I just shake my head dumbly.

11

"It's that you don't care at all," he says.

"And that's a good thing?" I say, puzzled.

It's as if he doesn't hear me, though. "You don't care about what I do at all, do you?" he says. "You never did. If I stopped playing basketball tomorrow, if I broke my leg tomorrow and could never play again, you wouldn't care about that at all. You never cared about any of that."

I open my mouth, but before I can say anything, he adds, "You only ever cared about me."

"I . . . You—" I get no further.

"I . . . You—" Ricky D'Amico, coming up on the other side of Danny, mimics me cruelly with a laugh. Then she does exactly what I'd like to be doing right then myself: She settles her butt, covered only by that Band-Aid breadth of shorts, down onto Danny's lap, drapes her arms around his neck possessively.

I don't even see it happen. I just feel it, as Danny slowly lets go of my hand, my hand left holding nothing.

Ricky D'Amico lowers her head, plants a series of kisses on Danny's neck, then looks up at me, a triumphant gleam in her eyes as Danny's arms rise up and encircle her.

"Didn't you realize Danny's here special for *me* tonight?" she says. "Don't you have somewhere else you need to *be*, Angel?" she says. "Aren't you supposed to be over by the *pool* with Karin?"

In a way I am surprised I give up so easily, but I tell myself that I will get another chance on another day, another night.

Still, I take my time drawing myself another beer from the keg, take my time walking away, take my time conceding, just long enough to hear Danny say in a hazy voice, "Hey, Angel, where you going?"

And maybe, I think, this is another reason why Ricky D'Amico has always hated me: She's a little bit in love with Danny Stanton too. Well, isn't everybody?

8:00 p.m.

"Hey!" shouts Tim O'Mara, practically in my face. "Can you believe we're going to finally be seniors this year?"

Tim O'Mara is one of those guys who is not really a dork—I mean, he got invited all on his own to Ricky D'Amico's end-of-summer blowout, right?—but who will never be at the top of anyone's A-list either. It's because of things like this, the way he says, "Can you believe we're going to finally be seniors this year?" The other guys, guys like Danny Stanton, can get rowdy all they want to and have it still sound cool, but when Tim O'Mara does the same thing, there is something just a little off about it, something a little too loud, a little too eager.

There was a time, maybe about a year ago, during one of the few times when I was really mad at Danny, that I thought I might like Tim O'Mara, like him enough to date him. He was cute enough, with curly blond hair and puppy-dog brown eyes, and he was certainly nice enough. Maybe that was it: Maybe he always seemed *too* nice. Whatever it was, I just couldn't pull the trigger. It was like it took too much energy to be around someone who was always trying too hard. Still, we always said hi if we saw each other in the halls, sometimes sat at the same table in the lunchroom, even had some fun together when we were partners in physics class.

Now, feeling as though I have lost Danny Stanton — at least for the night — to Ricky D'Amico, I find myself being warmer to Tim than I have been in a long time.

"Yeah," I shout back at him, nearly as loud as he has just shouted at me, taking a long sip off my beer, wiping the foam mustache from my upper lip. "It's great! Seniors!"

Before long we are shouting enthusiastically back and forth at each other about how great it's all going to be. Before long I am drinking more and more beer. Even though I know that, being so small, I shouldn't drink so much so quickly, I keep drinking with Tim O'Mara, the two of us getting louder and louder. We are like our own symphony of two, only with all false notes, every single one off-key.

At one point I look back toward the garage to where Danny Stanton was seated. *He is not used to me paying so much attention to someone else,* I think. Even if he may not want me all the time himself, he is not used to having me seem to favor someone over him. But when I look over, I see him rising from the chair, see Ricky D'Amico tugging him toward the house, see him trailing behind her, see the back door close behind them.

"Hey," Tim O'Mara leans in to whisper in my ear, except it comes out more like a bit of a shout anyway, "why don't we get out of here?"

9:00 p.m.

Tim apologizes for his car, a ten-year-old Volvo.

"It's my father's," he says, left hand on the wheel. He turns on the radio, and a second later I feel his other hand on my knee, then it inches up my thigh a bit. "He says there's no point in buying new before the old's totally worn out."

"Where are we going?" I think to ask, my mind hazy from all the beer, my tongue thick in my mouth.

I look over at him, see him smile in the glow of the dashboard light.

"Back to school," he says.

Five minutes later he is pulling into the parking lot of the middle school we both went to, so many years ago. He parks the car, clicks off the engine. Then he reaches over into the backseat and, after some fumbling around, turns back to me with the necks of two bottles of beer clasped in his hands. "Want one?" he asks. Not waiting for my answer, he flips the top of one, hands it to me. "Here," he says.

I think, *I should not be doing this.* I think of the D'Amicos' rule and how Tim should have gotten himself a designated driver tonight. I think of how I never

16

should have gotten in the car with him like this. But then I think of Danny Stanton with Ricky D'Amico — they are probably kissing, or more, right now — and I take the bottle.

I take a long swig, and all of a sudden I am a lot drunker than I was a half hour ago, the car around me starting to swim: not a nauseating swim, just a gentle swim like I'm being sailed away on something.

Tim reaches for a knob on the radio, cranks the tunes louder. The swim intensifies as Tim leans in to kiss me.

It is not bad; it is not great. It is just Tim: a guy I've known for years, a guy I've never felt much for one way or the other, at most a guy I feel vaguely pleasant around.

He starts to kiss me harder, his hand resting on the place beneath the hem of my shirt and my stomach. Then he leans across me, opens my door.

"Come on," he says, opening his own door.

"What?" I say dumbly.

"Let's make ourselves more comfortable," he says, coming around to my side of the car, taking hold of my hand, leading me out.

17

Tim gets a beach blanket from the trunk, leads me to the gently sloping lawn on the side of the school. I have a dim memory of being much younger here, of teachers taking us outside for class on the first warm days of spring. It feels weird to be lying on a beach blanket with Tim O'Mara on the same spot where Ms. Welch used to talk to us about how to use topic sentences in essays, Ms. Welch talking loud over the sound of the lawn-mower as the landscaper trimmed the grass, bouncing up and down in the seat of his old John Deere.

"It's such a hot night," Tim says between kisses. "Are you sure you need this shirt? And what about these pants?"

It seems like a bad idea even while I'm doing it, but the beer in me is so strong now, and anyway it doesn't feel like it's me doing it, it feels like it's just Tim doing it, and I keep seeing Danny Stanton and Ricky D'Amico, when I still see anything at all, together in my head.

Tim does more than kiss me, but I feel less and less aware of what he is doing as I lie with my back against the ground, vaguely registering the bite of mosquitoes on my legs. I don't know if it's so much that I don't feel like myself as it is that I don't feel like anything at all.

When he starts to take off his own pants, I rouse myself enough to object. I know that I do not want this, not like this.

"Oh, come on," he says, and smiles, the night behind him as he climbs on top of me. "I'll just lie here for a minute while you think about it."

But I can barely think of anything. Later on I will remember suggesting there were other things we could do than the thing he obviously had in mind. I will remember saying I didn't want to get AIDS. I will remember saying I didn't want to get pregnant. I will remember saying I'd never done this before.

"Come on," he says again, more softly now, reaching for his jeans. I hear a crinkling sound, see in his hand what I realize must be a foil-wrapped condom. "See?" he says. "You won't get pregnant. You won't get AIDS. And, hey, everyone has to have a first time."

Later on I will remember nothing of the act itself: not pain, not pleasure. All I will remember is the sensation of things slipping away from me and the exact way the stars looked, winking overhead.

10:00 p.m.

I do not even remember putting my clothes back on, the drive home to my parents' house.

It is as though I come to as we pull into the driveway and Tim kills the engine.

He reaches to kiss me again, but it is different from his earlier kisses. Those were like he was saying a different form of hello, like he was trying to reach for something; this kiss feels more like he is doing the last thing before pulling away, like he is shutting a door, saying good-bye. I notice he doesn't ask for my phone number, ask to see me again. This is okay: I would not want him to call, would not want to see him again, not like this. It will be bad enough passing him in the hallways at school when school starts up again.

"Hey." He smiles, mussing my hair. "It was great, right? You had a good time, right?"

I don't say anything to that. I am too busy feeling sick to my stomach, nauseous. But he doesn't let me go yet. Instead he laughs at what a "hard time"—as he puts it— I gave him earlier, the objections I raised before doing what we did.

"No one could call you easy, Angel," he says, and laughs.

Then he does an odd thing. He reaches over to the glove compartment, opens it, pulls out a small notebook and pen, writes something, tears off the sheet, hands it to me.

"Here," he says.

I look down at the scrap of paper, squint at the letters and numbers on it: "Tim O'Mara" and a phone number.

He reaches across me one last time, pulls the handle for me one last time, pushes the door open for me one last time, laughs one last time.

"Call me if you're pregnant," he says.

After I get out of the car, he pulls the door shut behind me as I walk toward my parents' house.

In four hours my life has totally changed: I have had sex for the first time, an act I do not even remember.

In exactly two and a half months I will use that phone number and I will call Tim O'Mara.

september

IT IS HARD TO BELIEVE THAT AFTER SO MANY YEARS OF schooling together, we are seniors now, this will be our last year in high school. From the day school starts, right after Labor Day, it is like we are all on a collision course with the future, riding high on a wave of energy, and living loud.

"Seniors!" someone shouts nearly every day, pounding the lockers as whoever is doing the shouting runs down the hallway. "Seniors!"

Sometimes it seems as though Tim O'Mara is shouting louder than anybody. Sometimes it seems as though every time I walk down a hall, there's Tim O'Mara, shouting, "SENIORS!"

We have not said a word to each other since the night of Ricky D'Amico's party. At the time I didn't expect him to call me—after all, he never even asked for my number. But as the days have piled up, I've been surprised that no call has come. I guess a part of me thought that Tim O'Mara, who has never been known to have a regular girlfriend, might take our one night together as an excuse to try to turn it into something more. Weird. Even though I have no interest in him in that way whatsoever, that part of me that half-expected a call, that part that had rehearsed in my mind how to let him down gently, is kind of hurt that the call never came.

More puzzling is that he hasn't spoken to me since then, even though we share some classes, even though we see each other in the lunchroom every day, pass each other in the halls all the time. He used to say hi to me a lot before, used to say it before I even had the chance to, as if he were worried that if he didn't say something to people each time he saw them, they wouldn't even bother to acknowledge him. But now he says nothing.

I try to tell myself it doesn't mean anything when he walks by me with a group of his friends and doesn't say anything as he stares at me, his friends staring too while they pound him on the back and give him high-fives. I try to tell myself it doesn't mean anything when I am sitting in the front row of our Law in Society class and I hear what sounds like my name — *Angel Hansen* — being whispered from the back of the room, and I turn in my seat, only to see Tim and his friends laughing.

I ignore everything because I just need to get through this one last year of high school. I need to get through Creative Writing and Law in Society and French IV and Calculus II and Oil Painting and Physics II and European History and even gym class. I need to buckle down and keep my grades up and study for the SATs, which I will be taking in five weeks, those all-important tests that serve as pearly gates, those tests that will decide whether I will be able to go where I want to go next year, rather than having to settle for whoever will take me.

So I cannot worry about Tim O'Mara and whatever he is saying; I can't worry about his stupid friends.

I am in the lunchroom, eating at a table by myself and wondering why no one seems to sit with me anymore, why there suddenly seems to be this no-fly zone around me now, when Karin practically throws her tray on the table and plops down onto the bench across from me.

"So," she says in a tone I don't remember her ever using with me before, "when were you planning on telling me, huh?"

"What?" Glad for the interruption even if her tone worries me, I put my cheeseburger down. On good days the cheeseburgers taste like something you wouldn't really want to eat, not unless you were in prison or high school, but lately they have started to . . . *smell* awful to me. At least now that Karin is here, I will not have to try to force myself to eat something that is making me feel so gross. "What are you talking about?" I ask again.

I can tell from the look on her face that Karin is really mad or maybe just very hurt. I have seen that anger directed at other people, I have seen her hurt when some guy she liked wasn't as interested in her, but I have never seen those things directed at me. The last time we even fought was freshman year when we both tried out for the basketball team, both sucked, and each blamed the other for not making the cut.

"If you had caught the ball when I threw it to you . . . ," I'd said.

"If you even knew how to throw a ball in the first place . . . ," she'd said.

25

We'd both wanted to be on the girls' basketball team because Danny Stanton was on the boys' team, and so was his best friend, Todd Ferris, whom Karin had a crush on. Neither of us were cheerleader material—we both lack the gene that enables a girl to scream at the top of her lungs and smile for three hours straight at a football game while freezing her ass off in a micromini—and so we'd figured the most efficient way to get close to Danny and Todd was if we shared a common interest: basketball.

But I can see from the look on Karin's face that whatever it is that's bothering her, it is way more important than basketball.

"When were you planning on telling me about you and Tim?" Karin demands.

"Oh," I say.

"'Oh'? That's all you have to say? 'Oh'?"

"There's nothing to tell," I say.

"Nothing to tell? I'm supposed to be your best friend, Angel. I thought we told each other everything."

"We do."

"Is that right? Then how come I'm the last to know? How come I only heard about you sleeping with Tim after I heard Ricky D'Amico and Dawn Peck talking about it in art class?"

So people have been talking about me.

"Look," I say, "I'm sorry. I didn't say anything to you about it because I was too embarrassed."

"Why would you ever be embarrassed about anything around me?"

"I was embarrassed because it was such a stupid thing to do. It was stupid of me to get so drunk, it was stupid of me to get in the car with Tim, and it was really stupid of me to do anything with him. *God*, I don't even remember most of it!"

"You had sex for the first time and you don't *remember* it?"

I shake my head.

"I told you the first time I did it," she says. "We promised each other we'd tell each other about the first time."

She's right. We did promise.

"I thought for sure you'd tell me," she says.

"And I would have," I say, "if it *mattered*. But it was so . . . so . . . so . . . *nothing*. It was like the least important thing I've ever done. It wasn't like I had something

27

important to tell you. I mean, it was like less than nothing. Does it even count as a first time, if I don't even *remember* it?"

And Karin surprises me: She laughs. And suddenly it is like she is her old self and there is no longer anything wrong between us.

"No," she laughs. "I guess that doesn't really count as any kind of first time at all."

"So," I say when she is done laughing, "people are really talking about me?"

She shrugs it off. "Of course," she says. "But I think that's just because everyone was so surprised. I mean, who would sleep with Tim O'Mara?"

She must see from the look on my face that this bothers me, because she leans across the table and whispers, "But don't worry about it. I'm sure people will get over it in about a week."

Week of September 10/Week 2

But people do not get over it. Or, at least, Danny Stanton doesn't get over it.

At the ring of the bell I walk out of art class, only to

find Danny Stanton making out with Ricky D'Amico, whose class follows mine, right outside the door. He has her leaned up against the wall, one hand resting on the narrow of her waist as he kisses her. From where I'm standing I prefer to think it's her trying to pull him closer, rather than the other way around, but I know this may not be so.

I start to head off to my next class. Then I stop, lean against the wall a few feet down from them, my back to them. It has been so long since I talked to Danny— usually he calls to say hey at least every few weeks, but lately he has barely nodded to me when we pass in the halls—that I decide to wait her out.

At last I hear the door to the art room get pulled shut by the teacher, hear Danny's steps from behind. As I look around, I see the hall is almost deserted now, nearly everyone else has gone on to his or her next class.

Danny has already walked past me when I say "Hey" softly.

He spins around.

"Oh," he says. "Angel."

"Walk with me?" I say. It is something we have said

to each other before. It is our own private signal that one of us wants to take a break from the idiocy that is high school all around us.

His eyes narrow.

"Don't you have another class to go to?" he says.

I shrug. "I was thinking of skipping." I shrug again. "Walk with me?"

"Sure," he finally says. "I guess I could skip. I'll walk with you."

We walk side by side through the deserted halls, not saying a thing.

Even though I was the one to suggest this, I have no idea where I want us to go. Which is okay, since Danny has no problem leading. He leads us into and through the cafeteria and out again, into one of the outdoor areas that kids hang out in when they have study hall or just want to skip. If this were back in my mom's day, kids would be smoking, because this outdoor area with the overhang, all concrete and brick, would be a designated smoking area. But this is not my mom's day, so kids have to wait until they get off school grounds to light up. Even though Danny plays basketball, he's been known to smoke from time to time, and I see him nervously pat at the pack in his shirt pocket before letting his hand drop when he remembers where he is.

I look at him and I think there's not another guy in the world that looks as good in a simple black T-shirt as Danny Stanton does.

"So," he says, and there's a weird slice of anger I hear in his voice, "we walked."

Now that I have him here, with me, I am not sure what I want to say.

"So," I finally fumble, "you and, um, Ricky have gotten pretty tight, huh?"

Instead of answering my question, Danny slams his hand against the brick wall right next to my head. It's so close, so sudden, I can't help myself: I jump.

"Your hand!" I yell, reaching without even thinking about it for the hand that hit the wall. The first thing I think of is those beautiful hands. In less than two months basketball season will start. And even if I do not care if Danny plays or not, *he* cares. He loves basketball, and I know he needs his hands to play.

But he ignores me, shakes my hand off.

"What the fuck is *wrong* with you, Angel?" he says, and it's almost a shout.

"What?" I say. "What are you talking about?"

"Tim O'Mara," he says. "*That's* what I'm talking about. What were you *thinking* of?"

But of course I can't tell him what I was thinking of that night. I can't tell him that I was so upset at the sight of him with Ricky D'Amico, I wanted so much for it to be me with him instead, that I stopped thinking at all.

"What's the big deal?" I say, getting angry myself. "It's not like you and I ever had any kind of promise between us. It's not like you don't go out with any girl you want to every chance you get."

And it's true. In addition to the so-called cool girls, like Ricky D'Amico, Danny has gone out with some real skanks over the years. And did I ever give him a hard time about any of that? Sometimes I see the double standards between guys and girls that my mom is always talking about, and it bugs the hell out of me.

"That's not the *point*," Danny says.

"Then what is?" I say.

"*Tim O'Mara.*" He gets up close in my face, emphasizes each word. "Do you have any idea what kind of a jerk that guy is? I mean, come on, Angel. Go off with some guy at a party, fine. But *Tim O'Mara*? Do you have any idea the things that guy's been *saying* about you?"

I stand my ground. This time, I get right in *his* face. And all the while I'm thinking of him and Ricky D'Amico. "And why should you care?" I say. "Huh? Why should you care?"

"You know something, Angel?" He takes a step back, puts his hands up in the air. "You're right. Maybe I don't care at all."

And then he turns and walks away from me.

Week of September 17/Week 3

"Your father and I have been worried about you," my mother says.

We have just been seated at a table at The Big Enchilada, which my parents know is my very favorite restaurant in the whole world.

My father asks if I want the grande nachos with beef or with chicken for an appetizer. Even though the very idea of any kind of nachos makes me feel sick to my stomach right now, I say beef. I know my dad likes the beef nachos better.

"It's just that you don't seem like yourself lately, honey," my mother says.

My mother, Helena Hansen, is still a very pretty woman. In pictures I've seen of her when she was younger, she was drop-dead gorgeous, with all of the long darkness of my hair but none of the frizz, a sparkle in her eye that marks her as the kind of girl anyone would want to know. My dad sometimes calls her "Hel on Wheels."

And my dad, Steve Hansen, is her match, even though he looks completely different from her. He is very tall, making both my mom and me look tiny when he walks between us, with hair that is still a sandy blond even though he is in his midforties, and blue eyes that are like chips from the sky. He still plays racquetball on his lunch hour twice a week, and my girlfriends, for as long as I can remember, have been known to develop crushes on him.

It used to bother me, my parents looking the way they do—like a supercouple who took a wrong turn at Hollywood and wound up living here—because I felt sort of guilty, as though nature had played some kind of cruel trick on them. When you look at their wedding

34

pictures, they look so perfect, you imagine they would have produced an equally perfect child. And while there is nothing incredibly awful about the way I look—I don't have a second nose growing out of my forehead or hair coming out of my ears—I am so average by comparison. Still, they have never made me feel anything less than totally loved, have never shown any real disappointment in me in any way, and over the years I have grown to accept the differences between us. I think, *If they do not mind the differences between us, then why should I?*

"What are you talking about, Mom?" I ask now. "Who do I seem like?"

"I don't know," she says, her pretty brow furrowed in a frown. "Just not yourself."

"Ease up on her, Hel," my dad says. "She's under a lot of stress." He studies the menu. "Do I want the shrimp fajitas or the chimichanga? Hmm . . ."

"Stress?" my mom says. "What kind of stress? She's only seventeen." My mom turns to me. "Angel, are you under any stress?"

"Well," I say, twisting my napkin a bit, "I guess maybe I am under a bit of stress. You know, the SATs are coming up next month, and my meeting with my guidance counselor is next week . . ."

"You'll do fine," my dad says. "Whatever you want to be in life, you'll be." He nods, as if saying yes to himself as he closes the menu. "Definitely the shrimp fajitas."

When our main courses arrive, I excuse myself to go to the bathroom. I lock the stall door behind myself just in time, lean over the toilet bowl just in time to puke my guts out, even though I haven't really eaten anything yet. Afterward I rinse my mouth out with water from the sink and splash cold water on my face, which has started to sweat. This is the second time I've thrown up this week, and I've also started to pee more frequently. It's as though every time I take two sips of something, I have to go.

Back at the table my mother studies me closely.

"Are you all right?" she asks.

"Fine now," I say. "I think I just got a bad piece of meat."

Her dark eyes narrow.

"You're not bulimic, are you?" she asks.

"Mom!"

"Sorry." She colors slightly. "Well," she says, "a mother has to ask."

"She just had a bad piece of beef." My dad gestures with his fork. "Happens all the time."

"We're just worried," my mom says, "because you never seem to go out anymore. Not that you ever went out every night, but you *never* seem to go out anymore. And I can't remember the last time we saw Karin at the house. . . ."

"It's just stress, Mom," I say, hoping to reassure her. "Everyone's just worried about getting into the right colleges. I'm sure Karin's just worried too."

When we get home, my father goes into the family room to turn on the TV. I know he will turn on Joe Scarborough and that soon he will be yelling at Joe Scarborough. My dad likes to yell at Joe Scarborough.

My mother stands in the kitchen, making out a shopping list for the next day.

"Eggs, whole wheat bread, ice cream." She keeps writing, not looking up. "Angel," she says, "do you need me to pick up some more tampons for you?"

I read an article once in a girls' magazine, about how girls who live in the same place—sisters, or roommates in college—find that they start getting their periods around the same time. It's like the moon lumps them

37

together in one slot. And this has proved true of me and my mother. She always knows that if she has just gotten her period, I will soon be getting mine as well.

In the top drawer of the desk in my bedroom, I keep a small notebook that I have kept since my mother gave it to me when I was eleven years old, the first time I got my period. In the left-hand column there are dates listed under the heading "Arrived"; in the right-hand column there are dates under the heading "Due." I have yet to write a new date down in the left-hand column, even though the last date in the "Due" column is some days passed now.

"Sure," I tell my mom. "I could use some more."

I figure that if my period doesn't come in the next day or two, I will still take tampons every few hours from the box under the bathroom sink, I will wrap those tampons in toilet paper, so that my mom won't worry that something is wrong, and I will drop them in the trash as if nothing has changed.

Even though, as I think that, I realize that every-thing has changed. My period hasn't arrived yet, my breasts have felt tender lately, my body is changing—there is a mild aching, a fullness in my lower abdomen, sort of as though my period is about to come, except it hasn't.

Whenever I think of those changes, my mind starts to scream in panic. So I don't let myself think of them.

Instead I tell myself these changes don't necessarily mean anything. I tell myself these changes, not to mention my missed period, must all be due to stress.

Week of September 24/Week 4

And of course I *am* living under a lot of stress. I am a high school senior trying to get into the college of my choice, trying to make the right decisions about what I want to do with the rest of my life.

"It'll be fine," Karin whispers as we stand in the hallway outside the open door of Robin Keating, my guidance counselor.

Karin knows everything about me, so she knows that I always get nervous about talking to authority figures, even if I'm not going to see them because I'm in trouble about something.

"You'll do great," Karin whispers. "Knock him dead."

Knocking him dead seems like it would be overkill, so instead I simply knock softly on the open door on which there is a poster that makes no sense to me: WASTE IS A TERRIBLE THING TO MIND.

"Enter!" booms the voice of Robin Keating.

Robin Keating is one of those breeds of schoolteachers or administrators who always wears an old tweed jacket with leather patches on the elbows and insists students call him by his first name. He is also kind of cute, in an older-guy sort of way, with thick brown hair that could use the services of a comb, and greenish brown eyes twinkling behind steel-rimmed glasses. There have been rumors for years that there is something more than counseling going on between Robin and Megha Parks, the most stunning girl in our class, but I don't buy it. I think sometimes people just like to make up nasty stories where none exist. Robin is too smart to get caught up in the kind of thing that could cost him his job, although I don't suppose I'd be surprised if they got together after we graduate.

"Ms. Hansen," he says, indicating the grey metal-backed chair beside his desk.

Even though Robin insists the students call him by his

first name, he always addresses us as Mr. or Ms. It is a peculiar quirk that sets people off balance, as though he wants you to treat him like an equal, while at the same time he will show you the respect you deserve—if not now, then the respect you will hopefully deserve someday.

I sit in the chair, books clasped close against my chest.

"So," he says, taking off his glasses and chewing on the arm, "it's finally that time, huh?"

"Excuse me?"

"Time to plot out your future, of course. Have you given any thought to where you want to go to college?"

I take a big breath. "Yale," I say.

He eyes my transcripts, which he has out in an open folder in front of him.

"I see," he says. "But are you sure that's . . . practical?"

"What do you mean?"

"Well, it's not like your grades are bad. They're very good, in fact. But they're not exactly what you'd call stellar. Where else are you going to apply?"

In the instant he asks that question, I make a decision that I didn't know I was going to make.

"Nowhere else," I say. "Just Yale."

He laughs softly. But if there's a joke here, I don't see it. "Not Harvard?" he says. "Not Princeton, too?"

"Just Yale," I say again.

"How come not the others?" he asks. "If you're going to shoot for the moon . . ."

I shrug. "I like Connecticut," I say.

"Fine," he says. "So. Connecticut. How about applying to some of the other schools in Connecticut? Maybe some of the other ones that won't be quite so . . . difficult to get into?"

"I don't want to do that," I say. "I want to go to Yale."

"Just Yale?"

"Just Yale."

"And what do you plan on studying at *just Yale*? That is, if you were lucky enough to get in there?"

I feel the nerves starting in my stomach again, because I am about to admit something out loud that I have never admitted to anybody, not even Karin. Even my parents don't know yet: If they did, they would probably try to talk me out of it, because it isn't practical and they both have very practical jobs, my father working as a lawyer, while my mother runs an accounting practice from our home. Just like with how different I look from them, this makes me wonder at times if I am really their daughter at all, or if I were left with them by gypsies, the choices we make are so different.

"I want to be a writer," I say. "I want to write novels."

"An admirable ambition," he concedes. "You do realize, though, that it's not like wanting to do other things, like being an accountant or a doctor, say. It's not the kind of thing where you can just say, 'I want to do this,' and then, if you get good grades in school, there's a definite job waiting for you."

I haven't really thought about it this way before, but of course what he says makes total sense, is about as true as anything anyone in authority has ever said to me. Still . . .

"It's all I've ever really wanted to do," I say, and that's true too.

"And it has to be at Yale?" he says.

I won't answer that question again. Instead I ask, "What do you think I'd need to do to get in?"

He glances at my transcripts again, laughs softly again.

"Well," he says, "a twenty-four hundred on your

SATs would help, although I can't imagine anyone getting a perfect score. But I still think you should apply to other places too, just in case."

I do not tell him what I know to be true: Every time I have truly wanted something in life—with the exception of Danny Stanton, of course—I have always been able to get it somehow. In fact, there have been times when I've wondered if I must really want Danny so much. After all, if I did, surely with enough determination I would be able to get him. I think this because of my history of getting what I really want. I wanted Karin to be my best friend more than anything, and I got her. And here is why I don't say any of this aloud to Robin Keating: It is because, with no other reason for it available, I have attributed my luck at getting what I really want to my name. I think my name is somehow lucky. It is the only explanation I see.

I suck it up. "No fallback position," I say. "Looks like I'll just have to get that twenty-four hundred on the SATs."

october

IT IS THE NIGHT OF THE ANNUAL SADIE HAWKINS DANCE.

Each year girls in our school ask guys to be their dates. Some ask guys they are already going out with, knowing they'll say yes. Some ask guys they would like to be going out with, hoping they'll say yes. Sometimes they get lucky, sometimes they don't. Each year Karin and I go as each other's dates. I prefer to go with her because the only guy I have ever wanted to ask is Danny Stanton, and he always seems to be going out with someone else around the time of the dance, some other girl who asks him first. Karin always prefers to go with me, because for as long as I have been nursing my feelings for Danny, she has been nursing a lesser crush on Danny's best friend, Todd Ferris, but she thinks it's dorky for girls to ask guys out. Todd is not quite as tall as Danny, not quite as athletic-looking, but most girls

45

find his shaggy blond hair and hazel eyes cute.

"What would I do if someone said *no*?" she always says. So we have always gone together, wearing the hickiest clothes we can find to fit in with the Sadie Hawkins theme — cutoff jeans shorts, rope belts, button-down checked shirts tied at the waist, straw hats.

And this year is no different.

Only maybe it is a little different, because this year it is a good thing that my checked shirt is so loose, since my breasts, still tender and now swollen too, have started to not quite fit in my bras. It is also different because as soon as we walk into the darkened cafeteria — where a band of our schoolmates who call themselves The Wrong Equation are playing a lousy version of an Eminem song, loud — Karin bumps right into Todd. He is hanging out at the ticket table, waiting on Danny, who is waiting on Ricky D'Amico, who is taking tickets and stamping hands. Ricky, who has managed to edge out Sherry Bixby as head cheerleader of the varsity squad, is on all the dance committees, and she will be taking tickets at that table for at least an hour, until her shift ends. Then she will be free to do whatever she likes with Danny.

"Nice outfits," Ricky says to us as she stamps our hands, her words as close as a person can come to a verbal sneer. "Who are you two supposed to be, Paris and Nicole on a bad day?"

When Danny sees I'm one of the two people she says this to, he looks embarrassed, looks away from me right away. I am not sure if he's embarrassed about what she said or embarrassed to know me.

And this is hard, because whatever else we have ever been, Danny Stanton and I have always been friends. Sometimes it has seemed as though we were best friends, a thing I would never tell Karin, of course.

But then Karin does a thing that surprises me, maybe surprising herself most of all. Even though she said she'd never ask Todd to be her date at the dance, she now does one of the boldest things I've ever seen her do: She asks him to dance.

"I know the band kind of sucks," she says, gesturing toward the dance floor, where the usual lunch tables and benches have been pushed out of the way, propped up against the walls, "but do you want to?"

And Todd surprises everyone, maybe himself most of all, by saying yes.

"Nice outfit," he says to her, taking her hand, only he says it in a way that is totally different from the way Ricky said it. When Todd says it, it sounds like he really means it, and as he looks at Karin, it looks as if he is seeing her for the first time.

I have always thought Todd was a bit of a jerk—I mean, he's no Danny Stanton—but when your best friend likes someone as much as Karin likes Todd, you have to try to see the good in that person. And I at least like the way Todd is looking at Karin now.

But once they are gone, there is no reason for me to hang out at the ticket table, and so I drift off, moving through the crowd, alone.

I talk to a few people that I know, complaining about this and that class, but there is no one I want to talk to for very long. Nor does there seem to be anyone who wants to talk to me for very long.

At one point I am standing alone with my back against the wall, thinking maybe I should be brave like Karin was, maybe I should ask some guy to dance, but there is no one I want to ask if I can't ask Danny, and that is when Joshua Carr comes up to me, asks me how I'm doing.

And that is when I know that I am really in trouble.

Not that there's anything wrong with Joshua Carr—he is even kind of cute, if overly clean-looking, with his short auburn hair and green eyes—it is just that Joshua Carr has a reputation for being The Nice Guy, meaning he talks to everybody, but he especially goes out of his way to talk to people that other people think of as losers, the ones no one bothers with. I have never known if this is some kind of religious thing with him. I have even thought before, often, that this is a very nice thing about him—whenever I've seen him trying to talk to someone so out of it, like the guy with the car fetish so extreme that even the other gearheads won't talk to him—but I don't want to be the object of anyone's pity. Certainly, I don't want to be the object of Joshua Carr's pity.

So when he asks me how I'm doing—do I maybe want some juice or a soda?—I tell him I'm fine, that I was just leaving anyway.

And that is exactly what I want to do: leave.

But when I locate Karin, who drove me, she is in a corner with Todd, who has one finger hooked in the rope belt on her jeans shorts while his other arm is

49

around her shoulders, with Ricky and Danny hanging close by.

Already Karin and Todd look like a couple, her head resting lightly on his shoulder like it belongs there.

"Hey," she says lazily, but not at all like she's unhappy to see me, "we were just thinking of splitting for the diner. Todd got too stoned before, and now he's got the munchies. Are you ready to go?"

I look at the group she is with and instinctively I know that by "we" she doesn't mean just her and Todd—which would just barely be tolerable, to be the extra person with her and Todd—but that she means the four of them, Ricky and Danny as well. Apparently Karin has forgiven Ricky her "Paris and Nicole" remark from earlier.

As Ricky smirks at me, her arm tight around Danny's waist, as Danny deliberately stares at some spot on the wall above my head, I just cannot take the idea of sitting at the diner, the place where everyone goes to hang out after ball games and dances, with Ricky smirking at me all night, with Danny carefully looking everywhere else but at me.

"That's okay," I say. "I think I'll pass. I was thinking

50

of heading home soon anyway, thought maybe I should get some more studying in before the SATs."

At that, Ricky snorts.

"So we'll drop you on the way," Karin says, and I can tell that even though she is where she has wanted to be for so long, with Todd, she is concerned about me.

"No, really," I say, forcing a smile to reassure her, even as I back away. "It's not on your way. I'll just call my dad."

Week of October 8/Week 6

Karin drives us to the SATs.

We have worried about and lived for this moment for so long, it is hard to believe it is finally here.

The room where we take the test is set up with square tables for four. Karin and I sit down across from each other at an empty one, but my butt barely touches the seat when I jump up again, hand over my mouth.

"What's wrong?" Karin asks, concerned.

But I can't answer. Instead I run out the door and down the hall to the bathroom, where I throw up

51

everything I had for breakfast: milk, juice, chunks of cereal—it is about as gross a sight as I have ever seen. I lean against the wall of the stall for a minute, feel the cool metal against my forehead. I wish I could just go home and go to sleep now—all I seem to want to do is sleep lately, I am that tired—but today is just too important. Unless I need to be rushed to the hospital, there will be no second chances, so I force myself to return to the testing room, will myself to fight back the nausea that never seems to be completely gone now. I will need to fight it for the next few hours, just long enough to do what I need to do.

"Are you okay?" Karin asks when I take my seat for the second time.

Before I can nod, she says, "What's that?" Then she reaches out with a finger, wipes near the corner of my mouth. "Gross," she says with disgust, wiping from her finger the fleck of vomit I'd missed. Then her expression softens. "Nerves, huh?" she says, and I simply nod, grateful to have a best friend who doesn't bail on me just because I got vomit on her finger.

Soon Todd comes in with Danny, and Todd sits down at our table as Danny moves off to find another seat.

I try to pretend that didn't just happen as I stare at the clock on the wall, waiting for the test to begin.

It is hard to believe that all our years of education finally boil down to this one test, that so much will be decided by the next few hours. I know that some in the room aren't worried at all, like Karin. Even though she has said she is nervous about this, I know she isn't, not really. Her grades are so good, she has prepped so much, she is bound to get what she wants. I know others are taking the test as a formality, that their futures are already decided and that those futures do not shine quite so brightly as Karin's.

For myself, I have studied hard for this. I know I need to jump through this hurdle to get to where I want to be. I have spent nearly all my time studying for the math part, math being my weakness. When I flipped through the pages of the English prep books, I realized that unless they changed things drastically, I could clear that part no problem. And the essay portion should be a cakewalk. If anything brings me down here today, it will be math.

Then, just two minutes before the test is to start, Tim O'Mara rushes in, late. There is only one available seat left, at our table, and he slides into the seat across from Todd, between Karin and me.

I don't even say hello. I cannot even think of Tim O'Mara right now. There is just too much riding on this moment in time.

I am still staring at the clock on the wall, watching the second hand move, my yellow number-two pencils lined up next to me, when the proctor says, "Turn over your test booklets and . . . begin!"

And now I am writing, writing for my life, it feels like.

My pencil flies down the answer sheet, filling in those tiny ovals with gray lead. I know all the English like I know my own name: It is as though the vocabulary section was designed with me in mind; the reading comprehension like a walk. When the proctor calls "Begin!" to start the essay section, I am much more relaxed, knowing I am capable of writing something that will rack me up those perfect eight hundred points easily. However, when the proctor later calls "Begin!" to start the math section, I am on less familiar ground, but I ignore the noise of people clearing their throats or turning pages around me, ignore the noise in my own head. My concentration narrows to the size of one thin dime as I call

up everything I have ever known about algebra, geome-
try, equations.

When the proctor calls "Time!" for the last time, I lay
my yellow number-two pencil down, feeling as though
I have run a long race. I am tired, but it is a good tired.

We get into Karin's car afterward, and I ask her how
she thinks she did.

"I think I did okay," she says modestly, and shrugs,
keying the ignition. "You?"

"I think I got an eight hundred on the English," I say.
"The essay part too." Then I let out a breath I hadn't
even realized I'd been holding. "And the math? I guess
I'll just have to wait and see."

Week of October 15/Week 7

The tension of the SATs behind me, it is tough to know
what to do with myself. True, I know that it'll still be six
weeks before I get the results, and true, I know that
there's still studying for classes to do, I still need to keep
my grades up, but I just can't concentrate on that. I
need to find something to take my mind off all of that,
take me out of myself, and so I decide to go to the mall.

"Do you want me to go with you?" my mom offers.

She knows I already asked Karin but that Karin said no, she had a date with Todd.

"That's okay," I say.

It's not that I don't appreciate my mom's offer, since I know she's been extra busy with work lately—a new client who forgot to pay his taxes for the last three years, even though he very publicly won a lot of money in a contest—but I would rather go alone. I am hoping to find some clothes to maybe reinvent my image— maybe a change of wardrobe or the right shoes will somehow make things better for me at school? And it is easier to shop for a new image when you are alone, when you don't have a mother along who is so used to seeing you in the old way that it is hard for her to see you as anything different.

"I won't be gone that long," I say. "Can I borrow the car keys?"

Driving to the mall, I see that some of the cars I pass have kids that I know in them, out for a good time. At the mall I see some others I know, clustered in groups at tables in the food court or looking in the windows of Limited Express. I wonder when life got to be like this for me, what has brought me to a point where I feel as though everyone else is part of a couple or a larger group, while I am here alone.

Without even recognizing that I am sad, I feel tears jump to my eyes.

It is so odd how emotional I am lately and how the littlest things can make me sad or angry or even happy. It is like being on a roller coaster of feelings with no memory of having paid admission for the ride. Certainly, there is no sense of control.

Immediately, impatiently, I wipe the tears away.

The mall at night feels strange. Even though it is not late, it is only about seven-thirty, there is an edgy quality to the air, like something could happen any minute. Everyone else is shopping with someone else, except for a few women who look like they could be mothers, walking fast from store to store as though they need to get their shopping in quick before the leash that is home yanks them back, and a few men in suits who look like they must be shopping for new shoes, making fast purchases at Mr. Boston or Structure and then grabbing a burger and fries at Nathan's before zipping off to the wife and kids or maybe a girlfriend.

I sit in the food court at a table alone, sipping a vanilla milk shake from Häagen-Dazs. I do not normally let myself have anything so big or sweet, but I have been feeling so nauseous lately and this is the only thing that appeals.

As I toss the empty plastic cup in the trash, I am bothered, as I always am, by the white noise lurking behind the piped-in music. It always feels to me as though I can hear that white noise, meant to hypnotize me, seducing—*Stay. . . . Shop!*—when all it serves to do is make me feel mildly irritated, as though there were a hornet in my brain.

I think I will do what the other girls here are doing, and I look in the windows of Limited Express, look at the accessories at Claire's. But somehow the idea of trying on the pants at the former, with their tight-fitting legs, doesn't interest me, and I already have enough cheap jewelry, so why bother with the latter?

Shoes, I think. *One of the things I thought I'd get here was shoes.*

But when I try on shoes in ALDO, in Steve Madden, even in Naturalizer, they don't fit properly. Even though I have asked for the right size—seven, my size—everything feels too tight, painfully so, and I realize that lately I have taken to wearing my sneakers to school every day because it has reached the point where they are the only shoes I own that don't hurt. I ask the salesgirl at Naturalizer to measure my feet, and she tells me they really are still a size seven.

"They're just a bit wide," she says. "They look a little swollen. Maybe you want to try a seven-and-a-half to accommodate the extra width?"

I shake my head, leave the store, and walk on.

I came here to get out of my head, to have a little harmless fun, but this shopping—shopping without finding anything I want or that fits properly—is only making me more tense.

Then, just as I am about to give up and go home, near the Macy's end of the mall I walk past a store I have never been in before or even noticed much: Mommy Heaven. *Well, of course I've never gone in there before or even noticed it,* I think. *Why would I ever go in there or even notice it?*

Yet now I am drawn to the display in the window.

I have, of course, seen pictures of my mother when she was pregnant with me. In them she looks as if she is growing an alien inside her, her frame normally so skinny that all you can imagine is that it almost *had* to have been some foreign force that did that to her. And here's the other thing: In those pictures she looks as if she has walked out of an eighties sitcom, her oversize blouses and dresses in shades of pink, and mostly with big bows tied loosely at the neck.

It is impossible to imagine clothes being more unattractive.

My mom and I have watched shows together sometimes, syndicated reruns of *Friends* where Rachel is pregnant, and at other times my mom has pointed out pictures to me of pregnant actresses on the cover of *Vogue* or *Vanity Fair.*

"Why didn't they have clothes like that when *I* was pregnant?" she has said. "I would have loved wearing those clothes. Instead I always felt like a big pink pod."

And I have known that she was right: She would have looked great in those clothes. She would have looked like the coolest pregnant woman ever.

And now here are the same pregnancy clothes my mom loves, here in the window before me, and they are every bit as cool as she thinks they are. There are jeans, just like the low-riders everyone else wears, low enough for someone to proudly show off a round belly rather than hiding it. There are gauzy tops with romantic sleeves, even halter tops. There are dressy dresses that even somehow manage to look sexy. I would wear those clothes.

At last I pull myself from the window, head for home.

I have no idea what I was doing there.

Week of October 22/Week 8

I miss my second period.

When I realize this has happened, my parents are out to dinner with my aunt Stacey and I am home alone.

I throw a minor fit.

I take the little notebook that I use to record my period out of my desk drawer and stare at the taunting "Arrived" and "Due" dates. Then I tear the most recent sheet out of the book, tearing every single used page out of the book afterward and shredding them, all the while with tears running down my face.

I am scared, more scared than I have ever been in my

life. And angry too, a part of me is so very angry.

At last, exhausted, I collapse on my bed, with my clothes still on. My mind screams, *What if there is something . . .* wrong? *What am I going to do?*

At last, I fall asleep, the tears still damp on my lashes.

When I wake in the morning, I tell myself it doesn't mean anything, that this is still just stress. Even though I have never been more than five days late before, certainly I have never been two months late before, I tell myself this is just stress.

It was just after my eleventh birthday that I got my period for the first time. My mom, usually so practical, was ecstatic. Never mind ecstatic, she was practically in tears.

"My baby!" she said, hands on either side of my face after I called her up to the bathroom, saying I needed a little help. "My baby is a woman!"

"God, get a grip, Mom," I said, trying to pry her hands from my face.

But she wasn't having any of that. She pulled me to her, wrapped me in her arms.

"Nothing will ever be the same after this," she said.

All the while I was thinking, *Of course things'll never be the same after this. Things are never the same after any moment.*

But, of course, I didn't say that to her. Mom was too busy having a moment of her own. We'd both been waiting for this for a year. Mom had told me she'd gotten her own first period when she was only ten, and this was one more thing that it seemed like she was better at than I was. I'd been waiting anxiously for this moment, she'd been waiting hopefully for this moment, and I decided to let her just enjoy her moment because the moment she was having was obviously way better than the moment I was having. But I did have to finally draw the line at . . .

"No, Mom, we do *not* have to have The Talk."

"But aren't there things you want to know?" she said. "You must have things you want to ask me."

"Actually? Um, no," I said, arms crossed.

But then, a minute later, seeing the wounded look on her face, I felt guilty.

"I'm pretty sure I know everything already," I said, trying on a smile, "but thanks."

"Everything?" she echoed.

"Well, Karin got this book, see, and really, it was very detailed."

"A book?"

"Great place to learn things, don't you think?" I said, really smiling this time.

"I guess," she said, not really looking convinced. Or maybe she was simply disappointed; maybe this wasn't the way she'd pictured things. She tried one last time: "Are you sure you wouldn't like to hear a little bit about the first time your father and I—"

"NO!"

Of course I didn't want to hear that kind of thing about my mother and father back then, and I don't want to talk to my mother about what is going on now. So I do not tell her about it when I start getting cramps, think I'm going to finally get my period, then realize that I have not gone to the bathroom to do "number two," as they say, in a few days, and realize that— gross!—I am constipated. Between the constant tired- ness, and the sore and swollen breasts, and the nausea and vomiting, and the increased urination, and now the constipation, it is as though some foreign army has invaded the body I once knew.

But I don't want to talk to my mother about any of this. So I keep taking tampons from the box under the sink at regular intervals, wrapping them in toilet paper, and throwing them in the trash as though business is as usual, even as the feelings of panic and doom in me grow each time I do this.

I do not want to talk to my mom about this because I know that if she finds out I haven't gotten my period in two months, she will tell me that my business is no longer as usual at all.

Week of October 29/Week 9

Even though we are seniors, even though we will be graduating in June and going off to college next fall, Karin and I decide to go out for Halloween one last time.

For the last few years we have gone to parties at friends' houses, but Karin says we should go out trick-or-treating this year, that we should dress up just like we did when we were young. I think, because she is my best friend, that I know what she is thinking: This will be our last chance to be someone other than who we already are.

We go to a little costume shop in town.

Karin rejects one costume after another. "I'm too old to be a princess," she says, "and I never wanted to be a witch."

At last she settles on a costume that makes her look like a rock star. There is a black miniskirt with a white halter top and a black leather jacket with chains on it, plus a wig with long black hair that looks like it could use a good combing.

"I'll wear it with black high heels and little red and white striped socks," she says. "Lots of makeup."

"Your legs'll freeze in that," I say.

"So?" she says. "At least I won't look like a dork."

Now it is my turn to look. But while Karin tried on several costumes before settling on the one she wants, I see only one costume that is right for me. It is on a hanger on a hook on the wall high up from the floor, and I have to ask the clerk to help me get it down. It is so high up, it makes it seem as though no one would ever bother trying to reach for it, because maybe no one would ever want it.

"What is that thing?" Karin asks.

It is a long rose-colored dress that looks like it came straight out of the nineteenth century, with a row of tiny buttons up to the neck, just the barest hint of lace on the sleeves.

"It's a dress," I say, feeling the fabric.

"I know that," she says, "but who are you going to be in it?"

"Jo March."

"Who?"

"Jo March. You know? Like in *Little Women*?"

Little Women was my favorite book when I was growing up—my mother gave me a copy for my tenth birthday—and Jo March was my favorite character in it. Jo was the odd-girl-out in her family, just like me, and wanted to be a serious writer, just like me.

"You realize," Karin says, "that no one will ever know that unless you tell them, right?"

"So?" I shrug. "When has anyone ever guessed my costumes?"

And it's true: Ever since we were kids, Karin has always picked recognizable costumes—Snow White, Alice in Wonderland, Cinderella—while I have always picked the weird ones: characters in books, like the time I was Rapunzel and everyone thought I was just your basic princess, or the time I went as my namesake from *That Was Then, This Is Now.*

Karin studies our reflections in the full-length mirror: her rock star next to my nineteenth-century writer.

"We sure don't look like we belong together," she says.

"So that'll keep it interesting," I say, thinking that on Halloween I will wear my hair up in a low bun at the nape of my neck.

And it is interesting when we go out on Halloween, interesting and fun as we walk down the streets, knocking on doors in a heightened state of giddiness. It is as though we are being kids again one last time before life gets serious on us.

When we knock on doors, some of the people who answer are surprised to see people as old as we obviously are still trick-or-treating. Still, I know from answering the door for my parents on a few Halloweens that you usually do get a few high schoolers, usually later on in the evening, though, and almost never in costume like we are.

Karin, of course, doesn't give anyone a chance to guess who I am.

"She's Jo March!" she tells everyone. And then,

when they only look at her with puzzled faces, she says, "You know? Jo March? Like in *Little Women*? God! Doesn't anyone in America *read* anymore?"

Our pillowcases are big, but we are young and full of energy and our legs are strong, and before long our pillowcases are nearly half-full.

We are still having fun — this is the most fun, the closest I've felt to Karin in some time — but there are only so many times you can knock on doors and say the same thing, tell the same joke.

"Want to go back to my place?" Karin says. "Get out of these things? Maybe get something to drink?"

On the way to her house we stop a group of younger kids who are still out trick-or-treating: two Harry Potters, Count Olaf from *Unfortunate Events*, Snow White, and the Wicked Witch.

"Here," we say, laughing as we take handful after handful of candy from our pillowcases, dumping it into their orange plastic pumpkins.

They look at us as though we might be trying to poison them.

"Take it," we say. "We didn't do anything to it."

"Don't you want it?" Snow White asks.

"No," Karin says. "We just wanted to dress up."

They look at us like we must be the craziest rock star and who-knows-what they've ever seen, but they take off fast down the road before we can change our minds.

We are nearly at the stoop to Karin's house, the walkway lined with candles inside little paper bags that have black cats on them, when I turn to her.

"I think I may be pregnant," I tell her.

november

I FINALLY GET UP THE NERVE TO TAKE A PREGNANCY TEST.
I go to CVS with Karin.

I call Karin to help me because: (1) she is my best friend in the world, and I know she won't tell anyone else about this, and (2) she has been through this before. Six months ago Karin went through the very same thing.

Karin helps me decide which kit to get. She says I should get one of the brands that have two tests inside, so that if I don't think the results of the first test are accurate, I can do it again.

When Karin went through this herself six months ago, she accepted the results of the first test right away. But she knows me: She knows that sometimes I need to hear a fact in class twice or see something proved twice before I believe it. Karin, who is Catholic, always says that if I were one of the apostles, I'd be Thomas.

My hand shakes as I take the pink and white test kit from the shelf, drop it in my red shopping basket. I figured when I grabbed the basket that what I was buying might not be so noticeable to the cashier if I was also buying a bunch of other things. So I walk around the store collecting other items. I put a big bag of M&M's in the basket, a can of Pringles, the largest box of Crayolas they have. It has been a long time since I used crayons. It has been a long time since I was young enough to care about coloring, but right now, seeing that box of ninety-six crayons in my shopping basket, all those pretty colors, all those perfect crayons still unused, comforts me.

Finally, we get in the short line to pay, and suddenly I feel as though I cannot go through with this. Karin must see the look of panic on my face, because gently she takes the metal handle of the basket out of my grasp.

"It's okay, Angel," she says. "I'll get it. My treat."

Karin doesn't even blink as she places each item on the counter, the last being the pregnancy test kit, doesn't blink as she gives the cashier her money, accepts her change, takes the bag from the counter and carries it out to her car.

Once inside her car I reach into my purse for my wallet, pay her back. She tries to wave the money away, but this is my responsibility and I keep my hand with the dollar bills in it held out until she finally accepts them.

I don't even hear the words of the songs that are playing on her car stereo, even though she has it cranked loud. And even though it is cold outside—it is November now, after all—I open the window, letting the icy air blow through my hair. I am so nauseous, it is as though I need that ice to keep me distracted from the desire to throw up.

Karin pulls into her driveway, parks in front of the stone house I know almost as well as my own. Ahead of time we decided—*she* decided for me—that this would be the best place for us to do this.

"It's always easier to stay cool about this kind of stuff," she said, "if you're not in your own home."

We go in through the back door, the bag with our purchases inside it now in Karin's hand, and I am momentarily thrown off balance when I see Karin's dad sitting at the kitchen table, reading through the day's newspaper as he sips from a bottle of beer.

"Hey, Angel!" he says, happy to see me.

Mr. Parker is always happy to see me. Sometimes he seems happier to see me than he does to see his own daughter. Karin has explained before that this is because he thinks she acts too smart all the time, that he thinks I—being more quiet all the time—am a good influence on her.

Mr. Parker eyes the CVS bag, his blue eyes dancing behind his steel-rimmed glasses. "What'd you girls get me?" he asks.

It is a good thing Karin is holding the bag, because if I were, I would probably have dropped it right then in shock and fear, letting the incriminating contents spill out all over the pale yellow linoleum floor.

Karin's smile matches her dad's in mischief as she peeks inside the red and white plastic bag, making sure the items don't show.

"Here," she says, reaching inside and pulling out the big bag of M&Ms, placing it down on the table.

"Aw, *man!*" says Mr. Parker. He waves the beer bottle. "That doesn't go with beer."

Karin checks the bag again.

"Crayons?" she offers, waving the box of ninety-six colors.

Mr. Parker shakes his head again in disgust.

"Then how about this?" Karin asks, producing the canister of Pringles.

"Hey!" Mr. Parker is happy now, reaches for the canister. "That's more like it."

Two minutes more of small talk and we are on our way up the short flight of steps to the second story. Midflight we run into Karin's younger brother, Kris. Kris is twelve and looks a lot like his sister, only not as tall yet, his hair just like hers, making him look just like the Little Prince.

"Hey," he says, "got anything for me in there?"

"Out of our way, squirt," she says, brushing by him.

Karin always says it's a pain having a brother, while I always say I think it would be great to have any kind of brother *or* sister. But much as I love Kris, as many times as I've wished he were *my* brother, I agree with Karin: Right now I want him out of our way too.

We go into Karin's own private bathroom, stopping only long enough in her bedroom to throw our coats, purses, and the Crayolas on one of her twin beds, lock the door behind us. It is the same lilac, green, and white bathroom she's always had, the same bathroom we stood in together on Halloween night just last week, helping each other with our makeup before going out. Yet somehow it all looks different to me now, changed.

Having locked the door behind us, Karin now second-guesses herself.

"Do you want me to leave?" She gestures vaguely toward the glossy white door. "Would you rather have some privacy?"

I shake my head. I don't want to be alone right now. Besides, Karin and I have been in that bathroom together many times in our lives. It was there we first experimented with makeup. It was there we first helped each other figure out how to use tampons. I would rather be with her right now than with anyone else in the world.

As she removes the thick foil wrapping from the first test wand, I drop my jeans and panties, squat down on the toilet, and wait as she reads the directions.

"Here." She passes me the wand. "I know it's gross and everything and it'll get all over your hand probably, but pee on this."

I accept the wand, do as she says, then I wipe it off, hand it back to her.

She places it on the counter as I stand up, pulling my panties and pants back on.

"It'll take three minutes," she says, looking at the clock on the wall, "maybe sooner."

We both look at the clock, look back at the wand.

Ticktock, ticktock.

The wand has just one dark pink strip in the little plastic window, same as before.

We both look at the clock, look back at the wand.

Ticktock, ticktock.

One of the three minutes has passed. There are only two more to get through.

We both look at the clock, look back at the wand.

Ticktock, ticktock.

A second line, faint pink, appears next to the first line in the little plastic window. It is amazing how quickly that second line darkens and thickens now, almost immediately matching the one running parallel to it in both color and size.

"Do you want to take the second test?" Karin offers almost immediately, starting to remove the thick foil wrapping from the second test wand. "Do you want to make sure?"

But I shake my head. For once in my life I do not need to hear the obvious facts twice, I do not need a second opinion, I do not need further proof. I now know what I realize I have known for a long time.

I am pregnant.

Week of November 12/Week 11

At last I make the call I need to make.

I open the top drawer of the white desk in my bedroom, the desk at which I usually do my calculus homework, my stories for creative writing. Underneath a story I haven't finished I find the wrinkled slip of paper I placed there so many weeks ago. Many times since the last weekend in August that slip of paper has resurfaced—like a fish you put back in the water that keeps coming back to bite at the line—whenever I've gone in the desk to search for something else. Each time, I've looked at the letters and numbers on it. Each time, I've thought of throwing it away. Yet each time, something has stayed my hand, and I've replaced the slip, burying it under whatever's on top.

Now I take the paper out of the drawer, study the

letters and numbers one last time before reaching for the phone on my desk, the phone that was a present from my parents on my twelfth birthday.

Hands shaking, I punch in the number, wait while it rings once, twice.

"Hello?" A woman, sounding not all that different from my own mom, only more severe, answers.

"Hi," I say, "is Tim there, please?"

"Who may I say is calling?"

"It's Angel." I cough. "Angel Hansen."

"Just a minute, please," she says, and I hear the sound of the phone being set down noisily on a table.

After what seems like the longest minute of my life so far, a minute that goes on so long I have time to reconsider, think about just hanging up the phone, I hear the clatter of the receiver on the other end being picked up.

"Hello?" Tim's voice says, cautious. "Angel?"

"Look," I say, before I lose my nerve again, "we need to talk —"

"Hey," he says in a hushed whisper that I can barely hear, before I can go any further. "I'm really sorry, okay? I know I shouldn't have said anything."

I'm surprised. "What are you talking about?" I say.

"I know I shouldn't have talked to the other guys about you, okay? But everybody saw us take off together from Ricky D'Amico's party, everybody wanted to know what happened. So what could I say? I mean, it was only the truth, but I know I should have kept quiet about it, kept my mouth shut. I know—"

"That's not what I'm calling about," I cut him off. "I don't care what you said to anybody about me." This, of course, is a lie. I mind very much that he told people what we did together, mind very much that everyone's been gossiping about me since school started. But right now that's the least of my worries.

"Then what—," he starts to say.

"I'm pregnant," I say, cutting him off again. "You said to call you if I got pregnant. Well, I'm calling. I'm pregnant."

"Holy sh—!" This time Tim cuts himself off. "Shit, Angel," he says, "that's too bad." Then he adds, "But it's not mine."

Now it's my turn to be surprised, so surprised that I raise my voice from the whisper I've been talking in, running the risk that someone else in the house will hear me. "What are you talking about?" I say. "Of course it's yours! Who else's would it be? You know I never did that with anyone else before! I haven't done that with anyone else since!"

"Shhh, shhh!" he says, hushing me nervously, as though he's worried that someone in the house on *his* end might hear my voice. "Okay, okay."

"Don't you believe me?" I say, hurt.

He thinks about it a moment too long before saying, "Yeah. Yeah, I guess I do."

"What are we going to do about it?" I ask, my tone quiet once again.

If a whisper can be said to shout, his does. "You're going to get rid of it, of course!"

And even though I don't like the way this conversation is going, don't like the way he speaks to me at all, I know he is right. This is what I've already concluded myself, before even calling. It is the only choice I have.

Maybe if I were older, I'd think about other choices, what other avenues might be open to me. Maybe I would consider keeping this . . . *thing* that is inside me. But I want to go to Yale, if I can even get in, right? I never want my parents to know this happened at all, right?

And right now all I can think is that I want this to be over, I want it to be as though it never happened at all.

There *is* only one choice for me to make.

In fact, I have been so sure this is the only choice I can make, that before calling Tim I called the abortion clinic, told them I was pregnant, got an appointment and the price.

I tell Tim the price now.

"Holy shit!" he says. "How much do you have?"

I have already decided about this, too. Sucking in a big breath first, I say, "You need to pay for all of it."

"What?"

"My savings account is held jointly with my parents. They're okay with me spending some on myself each week, but they want me to be responsible with it. It's supposed to be for expenses at college. They'll know if I take that big of an amount out. They'll ask questions. I can't have that. I don't ever want them to know about this. I'm the one who's going to have to go through this, it's my body that's going to have to go through this—the least you could do is pay."

I stop talking. This is the most I've said to him at once during this conversation, and I am suddenly exhausted, as though I've just finished giving an oral presentation in our Law in Society class.

"Okay," he sighs finally. "Okay. I'll get the money. I don't have it myself, so I'll have to get it from my dad."

"You're not going to tell him what it's for, are you?" I ask, panicked.

"Of course not. What do you think I am—stupid?"

Then he makes an arrangement to come by my house later that night.

My mother looks excited at dinner when I tell her Tim will be coming by. It has been a long time since I went out on a date, and I can tell she's hoping this night with Tim will turn things around.

But when Tim comes by at around eight p.m., he beeps the horn from the driveway. I come tearing down the stairs, still wearing the same clothes I had on that day.

"Aren't you going to change?" my mother asks. "Isn't Tim coming in?"

I give her an exasperated look that I hope conveys "I love you, but now we do things differently from the way you did them when you were my age."

"I already told you this isn't a date," I say over my

shoulder, hand on the doorknob. "He just wants to ask me some questions about, um, another girl."

"So couldn't he do that over the phone?" I hear, but I'm already closing the door behind me, flying down the stairs.

This time I have to open the passenger-side door of Tim's father's car for myself, and I collapse on the front seat, breathless.

"Here." He hands me a thick envelope. Not even a "hello"; just "here."

I take the envelope.

"Aren't you going to even open it?" he asks. "Count it?"

"No," I say. "I'm sure it's fine." And I am.

"Look." Tim coughs to clear his throat. "I'm going to go with you. When you go to have the . . . *thing* done, I want to be there."

This is so surprising, and I have been so much more emotional lately about, well, *everything*, that no sooner do I hear his words than tears come to my eyes. So far all we've talked about is the business, the mechanics of things. I thought it was only me going through the other part, the confused and emotional part, but now I see that

Tim is going through this too. It all involves him, too.

"That's okay," I say, touched by his concern. "Karin is going to take me. It'll be fine. I'll be fine."

And it is true that Karin will take me. Of course Karin will take me. She is my best friend in the whole world and she has been through this all herself, six months ago. She is, in fact, the blueprint for what I am doing now. Who else would take me?

Tim looks straight ahead out the front window. I follow his gaze, but whatever he's seeing out there, I can't see it.

He coughs to clear his throat one last time, still not looking at me.

"Then I'll need a receipt," he says.

"Ex*cuse* me?"

"For my dad," he says, still not meeting my eyes.

"*What?* You said you weren't going to tell him. You said that would be, and I quote, 'stupid.'"

"I couldn't help it," he says, squirming. "He wouldn't give me the money until I said what it was for. Anyway, he won't believe it really happened unless I go with you or unless you can get me, um, a receipt."

And then it hits me: Tim doesn't care about what

happens to me, about what I am going through. He only wants to make sure that this little bit of . . . *business* gets taken care of, and his dad wants a receipt so he can be sure I'm not ripping them off.

I am so disgusted, so thoroughly nauseated by this, and I feel so unclean, that I get out of the car without saying a word, slam the passenger door behind me.

Tim rolls down the window, yells, "Angel!"

I spin around. "Don't worry," I say. "You'll get your receipt."

Then I walk back into my parents' house, the thick envelope with the cash in it stuck into the back of my jeans like a revolver.

"That was fast," my mother says, looking disappointed. "Did you answer all of Tim's questions at least?"

"Oh, yeah," I say.

Week of November 19/Week 12

Karin pulls her car into a space on the street outside the abortion clinic, feeds coins into the parking meter. We have a plan: She has driven me here today, she will wait for me in the waiting room during the procedure, she will drive me home afterward to her house, so that if I'm not feeling well, I can just sack out on her bed until I recover, until I feel strong enough to go back to my own home. She will tell no one afterward about what we have gone through together today. She will keep my secret forever. It is a good plan, and one that is tried and true. We did the exact same plan, or at least the mirror image of it, when she was pregnant six months before.

Because I have been through this before with Karin, I know the layout, know what to expect. Because I have been through this before with Karin, I know to expect the protesters outside the clinic, know that there will be a gauntlet of right-to-lifers that I will have to run before going inside the doors. Even though the law ensures they stay a certain amount of feet away from the clinic doors, you can still read the words on their signs, still hear their shouts, still hear as the young man carrying the large Catholic cross prays loudly. Yes, I have seen all this before, heard all this before. But being a witness to someone else's life is different from having that experience become your own, different from living that life yourself. *Maybe,* I think, *it is the difference between being a bridesmaid and being a bride.* There's a big difference when you know that when someone yells, "That's a baby you're carrying inside of you! Please don't kill it!" they are yelling those words at you. I didn't take it personally when it was Karin they were yelling those things at, even though there was no way then nor is there any way now for the protesters to tell *which* of us is going in for the procedure, but I take it personally now.

Abortion is a perfectly legal medical procedure in this country, and the right to protest is a protected right in this country, but I know that if I were going to the dentist to get a tooth pulled, I would not be greeted this way.

Six months ago it was me holding on to Karin's elbow, steering her path, offering her support. Now it is her hand on my elbow. So perhaps the protesters *can* tell who is doing what here after all.

When we check in at the front desk, a part of me expects the woman seated there to deny my right to do what I have come here to do. Maybe she will say I am too young, that I need my parents' consent, maybe she will judge me. I do not know what I will do if this happens. But we do not live in a state that demands parental consent, and there is no judgment in her expression as she does her paperwork; if anything, there is a form of mild sympathy, like I might see on my mom's face after receiving an unfair mark from a teacher.

Of course, first they want to do their own pregnancy test, just in case I did something stupid when I did it at home, like maybe I could have made a mistake about those two pink lines. But of course the results are the same. *It would be nice,* I was thinking while waiting for them to examine my urine sample, *if someone were to come in right now and tell me I'm wrong, if someone would take this cup away from me.* But of course the results are the same. They ask when my last period was, and I tell them. I am not just a little bit pregnant, they tell me; I am very pregnant.

"Another week or so," says the nurse with a smile that is not unkind, "and we wouldn't be able to take care of this so easily for you. Another week or so, and you'd be past the first trimester."

"Trimester." What an odd word to hear in this context. It sounds like something having to do with school. And "first trimester": that sounds like something for which there must be a "second trimester" and a "third trimester."

"I guess it's just my lucky day," I say, trying to force a smile that just won't come.

The nurse sends me back to the woman behind the front desk, so that I can pay for the procedure in advance. I hand over my money—*Tim's* money—and ask for a receipt.

"Most people don't usually want one for this," she says.

"I need one," I say as she pulls out a pad, puts numbers on it.

Then she tells me to take a seat in the waiting room, where Karin is.

Even though it is first thing in the morning, the waiting room is already full. The women are all ages. Some look sad, some look nervous or scared, some flip through magazines as though waiting for nothing more important than a routine cleaning at the dentist.

Karin takes my hand briefly, smiles at me for strength, and I remember from being here with her before what will happen next: Soon, someone will come and divide us into groups. They will take us to rooms where they will explain exactly what's going to happen, give us a chance to talk about what we are going to do, make sure this is what we really want.

"It's not as bad as it sounds," Karin told me after she went through it. "It's not like they try to talk you out of it or anything. They just want to make sure you know what they're going to be doing before they start, and that it's what you want."

You have a choice between a general anesthetic that puts you totally out and a local anesthetic, where you're just numb from the hips down. I have chosen a local anesthetic because (1) it is not my money I am spending, (2) it takes longer afterward to wake up and recover from a general anesthetic, and (3) I have always been good with pain. If there is a little pain, or even a lot, I can stand it.

I know, from what Karin has already told me, that after the procedure we will be taken to a recovery room where there are beds but also lounge chairs not unlike the one my father has in front of the TV, the chair my mother hates, for us to lie and sit on while we recover. The nurse will give us orange juice to get our energy back, and they will let us stay as long as we like until we feel strong enough and able to go home.

I wonder if anyone has ever tried to stay the night afterward, if there has ever been anyone who, afterward, simply couldn't go home.

My group is called, and about six of us are led to a small room where exactly what Karin has described happens. As I listen to the nurse describe the upcoming procedure, I am surprised at the range of ages around me. Some are even younger than I am, and there is one woman in her twenties who looks like she is about to burst into tears any minute. At one point she turns to me. "You're so brave," she says. I do not feel brave, but I want to make her feel better. "It'll be okay," I say to her. "You're going to be fine." There is even a woman who looks like my mom's age, maybe a bit older.

Everyone has her own story.

The girls younger than me have the same story, my story: They made a mistake, want to correct it.

The teary-eyed woman says it's her boyfriend who wants her to do it. "He says we'll get married someday," she says, "but that we're just not ready for *this*."

The woman who looks to be my mom's age or older is the calmest of all. "I already have five kids," she says. "I love them, but I just cannot have one more."

I do not tell my story.

Now that we have been talked to, now that we have been given the chance to ask any questions we still might have, we are shown to changing rooms—little cubicles with only a curtain to pull across the top—and told to remove our clothes, put on the hospital gown with the opening in front. Then we are to wait our turns.

It seems like I have been waiting forever when the nurse finally comes to get me. And what have I been thinking of while I have been waiting? Nothing. My mind is blank. It is a room I have shut the door on, not wanting anything to get in or out.

The nurse leads me down the hall to a room, has me climb up on the table, place my feet in the stirrups. She is very nice, even squeezes my shoulder once between her bustling around.

The doctor comes in, and he is a very friendly man who looks a lot like my grandfather Hansen, who is only sixty-two. It makes me wonder what Grandfather Hansen would think if he could see me now, but I shut the door on that thought too.

"And how are you feeling today, Angel?" he says jovially, scrubbing his hands, snapping on gloves.

"Okay," I say.

"Let's take a look here," he says, squatting down on a chair between my legs.

I am about as embarrassed as I have ever been in my life, and I stare up at the ceiling, counting the tiles.

"This should be no problem at all," he says finally. "Before you know it, we'll have you out of here and back to your life."

I see the nurse come at me from the side, a long needle in her hand.

And then suddenly that door I've shut in my mind cracks open, then swings open wide to a flood of images.

I see myself at Ricky D'Amico's party, back in August, *reacting* to Danny going off with Ricky by getting drunk, I see myself *reacting* to Tim's invitation to get out of there by going off with him. I see myself *reacting* upon learning that I am pregnant, by mindlessly doing exactly what Karin has done before me, blindly following the trail she has blazed. Even when I called Tim about it, when I got upset by the harshness of his words—"You're going to get rid of it, of course!"—I *reacted* to his words by telling myself that, awful as the way he put it was, it was the only choice I had. *Reacting, reacting, reacting.* Everywhere I look in my memory, I see myself reacting to what is happening to me, rather than making a deliberate choice. And I see now, for the first time, that there is not just one path, that there are other choices.

"No," I say, trying to rise.

"It's all right," the nurse soothes. "A lot of strong people are scared of needles."

"No," I say again, with more force this time, successfully struggling up to a sitting position, removing my feet from the stirrups. "I've changed my mind."

I have gotten to where I am without really thinking, but I cannot do this without thinking. It's just not good enough to do this because other people do it, it's not good enough to do it because it's the easiest thing to do. I can't just do this without knowing if it's what I really want.

I know that if I go through with this now, this abortion, I will regret it later; there will be no taking it back, no do-overs.

I regret so many things already: being with Tim, letting myself get so drunk I don't even remember being with Tim.

This is not going to be one more thing I will regret later.

Whatever else may happen after this moment, and

I'm not even sure what I *want* to have happen after this moment, I know that *this* is not what I want.

I know it will be hard, but it is my choice. So many things that have gone before were not my choice. But this is my choice now. It is what I choose to do.

Week of November 26/Week 13

I help my mom prepare for Thanksgiving dinner, fighting against the waves of nausea that the smell of cooking food now provokes. I have still not told my parents that I am pregnant, nor have I decided yet whether or not I will keep the baby. Mostly, when I think about it, I think that I will probably give it up for adoption. I have not decided yet. It is something I need to think about some more.

So far I have managed to avoid telling Tim anything. I called him when I got home from the clinic, told him I wanted to get through the holiday first, that afterward I'd meet him to give him his receipt.

Of course, I have a receipt, but I didn't do what the receipt is for.

Nor do I have his money.

When I changed my mind that day at the clinic and went back to the lady at the front desk, she told me I couldn't have the money back.

"But I didn't have anything done," I said.

"But you made the appointment," she said, "and showed up. If you hadn't, we could have given the appointment to someone else."

I suppose I could have argued with her some more, but I figured she was right. Maybe this was just like any other service profession, like when you make an appointment with the dentist and then if you don't cancel it at least twenty-four hours before, you still get billed. Anyway, at that point I just wanted to get out of there.

"Have you done the potatoes yet?" my mom asks.

"I'm just about to," I say, plugging in the hand mixer. Before I turn it on, I hear the sounds from the living room: my dad talking to my grandfather and grandmother Hansen, to Nana and Papa, my mother's parents. I hear my three aunts and two uncles, my cousins, all against the backdrop of the football game playing on the TV.

It is the same every Thanksgiving, every Christmas: Everyone comes here because, even though my mother works so hard at her job and complains about the extra work of hosting the gatherings, Mom is the only one in the family blessed with the Martha Stewart gene. Even though she complains every holiday, I can always see her satisfaction when she looks up from her seat at the foot of the table and sees her pretty centerpiece, sees everyone's plates filled, everyone talking and laughing.

I turn on the hand mixer, and underneath its loud whirring noise I imagine I hear Karin's voice from the week before, when I came into the waiting room of the clinic about two hours before she expected me.

"What happened?" she asked. "What are you doing?"

"Let's go," I said. "I changed my mind. I can't do this."

"But you have to," she said.

"No," I said. "I don't."

"What are you going to do?" she asked, her voice sounding more desperate than even I was feeling, as I led us back outside, out into the light of the cold November day.

"They gave me some literature to read and a number to call if I didn't want to go see my regular doctor," I said. "They said I've already missed three months of taking" — I paused over the unfamiliar words — "*prenatal vitamins* and that I'd better see someone before too long."

"Then you're going to —" She paused, let the words hang there.

"Yes," I answered her unfinished question. "I'm going to have it."

Karin got into the driver's seat of the car, turned on the ignition, didn't say anything.

For as long as I can remember, for as long as our friendship has gone on, Karin has always been supportive of me. So it feels weird that, ever since that day, there seems to have developed a certain coldness between us. At first she called every day on the phone, asked me what I was going to do, asked if I'd told my parents yet; even though we talk every day at school, I guess she feels it's too risky to talk about it there. Each day I have told her I still plan on having the baby. Each day I have told her I haven't told my parents yet.

This morning there was a football game at school, the annual Thanksgiving Day showdown between our school and a rival town — we always lose — and Karin wanted me to go with her, but I said no. I just couldn't face the idea of seeing Danny Stanton and Ricky D'Amico together, couldn't face the thought of maybe running into Tim O'Mara, couldn't face the thought of seeing everyone's lives going on as if nothing were different.

I turn the switch off on the hand mixer, put one finger into the creamy white mixture inside the big green bowl, taste it to see if I've gotten the consistency right, if it needs more salt or butter.

"You'd better be careful with those extra tastes," my mother cautions.

"What do you mean?" I ask.

She reaches out and does the kind of thing only a mother will do: She inserts one finger inside the waistband of my dark purple skirt. It's a tight fit.

"I can remember when that skirt was loose on you," she says. "Not that I mind if you gain a little weight," she adds hastily, obviously not wanting to offend. "I always thought you were too skinny before anyway, but I know how you girls today worry about every pound."

I realize she is right: My clothes are getting tighter and I'm going to have to figure out something to do about that.

"I made the mistake of putting it in hot water in the wash," I say, feeling the blush of the lie in my cheeks. "I think it must've shrunk a bit."

Then I take the bowl of mashed potatoes out into the dining room, set it down on the table. I help my mother carry everything else out: the regular salad, the three-bean salad, the two bowls of stuffing, the gravy, the canned cranberry sauce that everyone will eat and the homemade cranberry sauce that no one will eat. My mother carries in the turkey herself.

After everyone is seated at the table, after everyone has whatever they want to drink—wine, beer, soda; I have milk, because I have read the literature they gave me at the abortion clinic about having a baby, and a glass of water—my dad starts carving the turkey right at the table, just like he does every holiday.

Grandfather Hansen says, "Angel, tell me, how did your SATs go? Did you get your scores back yet?"

When he talks to me, his face reminds me so much of the doctor at the clinic that I have to push the image away before I can answer him. I tell him I did and that my scores were better than I'd hoped.

It was not the perfect twenty-four hundred that

Robin Keating had jokingly said I needed, but it was close enough: twenty-two hundred.

"So?" Grandfather Hansen raises his wineglass to me. "Yale?"

Even though we have nearly all college grads among my parents, uncles, and aunts, even though all my cousins are already in college and some plan to go on to grad school, I am the first on either side of the family to have a shot at an Ivy League school.

I raise my glass of milk in Grandfather Hansen's direction, acknowledging the toast he's offering. "That's the dream," I say.

Before he asks me if I still plan on studying English — a course of study he obviously feels is a waste of time, which makes me thank the stars he doesn't know I specifically want to study writing — my dad finishes carving the turkey and we pass the platter around, filling our plates with this last item.

"Angel?" My dad looks to me. "Grace?"

As the youngest this has always been my job, a job that has frequently embarrassed me. We are not a very religious family — "nonpracticing" is what you would call us — but Mom and Dad like for us to make this gesture on holidays, and it falls to me to do so. In previous years I have skated by with mumbled thanks, sometimes nothing more than, "God is great, God is good, we humbly thank you for this food," sometimes saying something as little as, "Rub-a-dub-dub, let's eat the grub," Grandfather Hansen's personal favorite.

I bow my head over my clasped hands now and for the first time in my life feel the seriousness of the moment.

"Thank you, God," I say, "for everyone who was with us in the past, for everyone who is with us now, today, for everyone who is yet to come. Amen."

december

I GO TO SEE THE DOCTOR THAT THE WOMAN AT THE ABOR-
tion clinic recommended. This time I drive myself. When
I told Karin I had made the appointment, she offered to
go with me, but I told her that it was okay for me to go
alone. Somehow I sensed her heart was not in the offer—
things have been so different between us lately, so
strange and changed—and, anyway, I just feel better
about going for the first time alone. I will pay for it with
money from my savings account. I know my parents will
ask questions about the withdrawal when the statement
comes, I know I will eventually have to tell them what is
going on, but today I want to do this on my own.

As I drive to the doctor's office, I am aware of how
few times in my life I have ever done anything of impor-
tance by myself. Whether going to the abortion clinic or
shopping for something cool to wear to a party, someone

104

has always been with me—my mother, Karin, sometimes my aunt Stacey. Even when I took the SATs, I may have been taking them alone in that it was me filling out the answers, it was me who was responsible for what I did, but there was still a whole roomful of people around me, all sharing a similar goal: to not be complete failures, to maybe even have a little success. So this is the first time I am doing something like this alone.

But then I realize I am not alone. There is another life growing inside me now. And even if at times it is hard to wrap my mind around that startling fact, even if it is nearly impossible to believe that before too much more time has passed I will have a child, it is the greatest shock of all to think that I am not alone in this.

I don't know why, but just like the day at the abortion clinic, I keep expecting everyone at the doctor's office to be mad at me, keep expecting them to judge me.

But the nurse is very nice as she weighs me—I've only gained six pounds since this all started, which she tells me is normal for some people, what with the nausea and all—and takes my blood pressure, asks me the date of my last period. And the doctor, Dr. Caldwell, who turns out to be a woman, is very nice too.

Or at least she is very nice after we get over the first hurdle.

"So what took you so long to come in for your first appointment?" she asks sternly. "Don't you know it's important to start on prenatal vitamins as soon as you know you're pregnant? Don't you realize how important it is for you to see a doctor regularly for the sake of the baby?"

"The baby." This is the first time someone has spoken those words aloud to me.

Dr. Caldwell is very short, even shorter than I am without heels, and has short hair dyed red. She looks to be in her midforties and wears tortoise-framed glasses on a chain around her neck, her eyes a warm shade of brown.

"No," I say, "I didn't realize that. I've never known anyone who had a baby before."

And this is true. My older cousins haven't had kids yet, I have no brothers or sisters, and sure I've known girls at school who got pregnant before—Karin, for one—but none of them ever went through with the pregnancy.

"Well," Dr. Caldwell says, "it's very important." She

sits down at the little gray counter attached to the wall, scribbles out a prescription.

"Here," she says. "You can get this filled at the pharmacy after we're done today, start taking them right away."

"I guess I wasn't sure before," I say, "that I was even going to have . . . the baby. I thought I was going to just . . ." I let my words trail off.

"I see," she says. Then she smiles, pats the examination table beside me. "Let's get a look at you, see what we've got here."

I stare at the ceiling as I feel the fingers on one of her hands move inside me, feel as she presses down on my lower stomach with the fingers of her other hand.

"Everything feels perfect," she says, removing her fingers, snapping off her rubber gloves, tossing them in a waste receptacle. She looks at the chart with the information the nurse filled out earlier. "I'd say you're about fourteen weeks along. We'll give it a due date of June third."

For some reason hearing an actual date, a date for when the baby is due, makes it all seem more real.

She asks about my eating habits. I tell her I've been

having trouble keeping food down, but that my mom has always been a stickler for balanced meals.

"That's good," she says. "As for the nausea, hopefully that'll pass now that you're into your second trimester, although it doesn't always. It's hard when someone's as tiny as you are." She indicates the short span between my breasts and hips. "There's just not that much room in there for the baby to grow. Sometimes tiny mothers like you get a lot of heartburn throughout the pregnancy."

Then she asks me about alcohol. Do I drink? Take drugs?

"I never liked drugs much," I say, an admission that would have made me feel uncool to say it in school but that makes me feel relieved now. "And I've been so nauseous since . . . *this* started, I haven't had any interest in drinking at all. In fact, the last time I had a drink was the night that . . ."

"That's good." She drops her words brightly into the void left by my trailed-off speech. "Just don't start again now."

"I don't think there's much chance of that," I say. Then: "Doctor?"

"Yes, Angel?"

"The fact that I . . . waited so long before coming to see you—will that harm the baby in any way?"

"I don't think so," she says. "You know, I probably shouldn't be telling you this, but for years, before we had things like prenatal vitamins, women had their babies and mostly it turned out just fine. Still, modern technology and science are wonderful things. So now that you *do* have the prescription"—she taps me gently on the leg with the chart—"don't forget to take them."

She must see from the look on my face that I'm still worried, still concerned my not coming to see her earlier might have put the baby at some kind of risk. And it is weird to be feeling like this, since a dim part of me feels as though if some kind of accident were to befall the baby now, not something I'd chosen to do but something I had no choice or control over, it would save me from having to go through what I am going through now. I could just go back to my regular life with nearly no one the wiser.

"Don't beat yourself up, Angel," she says softly. "Human babies are remarkably resilient little creatures. There's no reason to believe that anything will go wrong with your pregnancy or that your baby won't be born just fine."

She reaches into a cabinet over the sink, pulls out a large paperback book that she hands to me. The book is called something obvious like *Your Baby and You*.

"This should tell you a lot of what you need to know," she says, "about how the baby is growing and changing inside you, about what to eat and what to avoid, even how to wipe yourself properly when you go to the bathroom in order to prevent infection."

"Is this all I need?" I ask. I'm used to having to read so many books for different subjects at school, it's amazing to think I can have a baby with reading just the one.

"Well," she says, and smiles, "if you want to make yourself really crazy, you can always get the bible all the mothers like to get, *What to Expect When You're Expecting*. But why make yourself crazy if you can avoid it? And, of course, as time goes on, you'll probably want to look at a few baby-names books. Most people usually do."

Baby names.

But I haven't even decided yet whether I want to

keep the baby or not. Sometimes it feels like this is all moving so slowly, like watching someone else's car wreck. Other times it feels like everything is moving too quickly for me to even make proper decisions.

Dr. Caldwell tells me to make an appointment at the desk for a visit in about a month. She says for now the visits will be monthly, but as we go along they'll become twice a month, then every week, then maybe even every day at the very end.

"Have you thought about what kind of delivery you want?" she asks. "Have you thought about Lamaze?"

I shrug my shoulders. "I hadn't really thought that far ahead," I say.

"You don't need to decide today, of course. Just take your time and read that book I gave you. Decide what you want, how you want it to be."

"Okay."

"Angel?" She has one last question for me.

"Hmm?"

"Have you told your parents yet?"

I shake my head.

"Not that it's any of my business," she says. "My only business here is taking care of you and that baby. But you might want to consider telling them soon. Before too long"—she looks at my waist, slightly thicker than it was three months ago—"your body will tell them for you."

Week of December 10/Week 15

But before I can tell my parents, I need to talk to Tim.

I call him and tell him I want to meet him at the diner.

He says, "What's wrong with meeting in your driveway, like last time?" He says, "What's the big deal, if all you're going to do is give me a receipt? It's sure taken you long enough."

The diner is about as public a place as there is in our town. It's the place kids go to hang out after school, after games. It's the place parents take their young kids for cheap food that they can pretend is better than McDonald's. But I do not care about that right now. Everything, so far, has been on Tim's terms. This, I decide, will be on my terms.

Dr. Caldwell said the nausea might pass soon, but it certainly has not passed yet, I realize as the odor of old grease slaps me in the face when I enter the diner.

The pregnancy book Dr. Caldwell gave me had a

number of chapters on the second trimester, which I am now in. The book said that the breast tenderness might decrease, which it has; that the nausea might disappear, which it hasn't; that I might experience leg cramps, back pain, pelvic ache, and hip pain, stretch marks and other skin changes, hemorrhoids and constipation, heartburn, nosebleeds and bleeding gums; and that while my breasts would be less tender, they would also become larger, the veins would be more noticeable, the nipples would grow larger and darker, there would be small bumps around them, and I might even get stretch marks there, too. I have had preliminary glimmerings of many of these symptoms and I find all of it gross. But one other thing the book said would happen was that the fatigue I'd been feeling for the past few months would disappear, and in this the book is right. As I enter the diner to have my talk with Tim, I feel more awake than I have in a long time; certainly, I feel stronger.

Tim is already there, I see, in a booth in the back corner, and I slide into the red leather bench across from him.

Tim has a large coke in front of him already, with more ice in the glass than coke, and a large plate of fries. On the fries there is no ketchup, just so much salt that you can see the tiny white crystal rocks of it glistening atop the grease of the fries.

"Want one?" He waves a fry at me in offer before popping it whole into his mouth.

Believe it or not, with the exception of the night he came to my parents' driveway to give me the money, these are the first words he's spoken to me face-to-face since the night of Ricky D'Amico's party in August. Not even a "Hi" in the hallways. Just those snickers from the back of the room.

I shake my head, no, the last thing in the world I want right now is a french fry, and the other last thing in the world I want right now is anything from Tim O'Mara.

Nervously Tim wipes the salt and grease from his fries on the legs of his blue jeans, reaches one hand across the table.

"Let me have it," he says. "You have no idea what a hard time my dad has been giving me about this."

"I don't have it," I say simply.

"What?"

"I don't have a receipt," I say.

"Come on, Angel, don't mess with me. You should hear my dad. He's even been threatening to tell my mom about this."

I just stare at him, but he misreads my stare as fear.

"Don't worry," he says in a hushed voice. "He'd never say anything to my mom about this. He's even more scared of her than I am."

"I don't have a receipt," I say again evenly, "and there's not going to be any receipt."

"Hey," he says, getting angry, "you promised me and I promised my dad."

I lean across the table and speak the words slowly so there will be no mistaking every word.

"There isn't any receipt because there's no point in giving you the receipt. I didn't have the abortion, and I'm not going to."

"You can't mean that!" Tim says. He has shot back in the booth seat so that now he is leaning as far away from me as is physically possible. It is as though I have shot him. It is as though it is the next-to-last frame in a cheap horror movie and the monster he thought was gone has just sprung back to life.

"Yes," I say, "I can mean that. I do mean that."

He is calmer now. I can see that he is trying to make himself appear calm.

"I gave you all that money," he says. "Where's the money?"

"I don't have it," I say.

Tim surprises me with what he does next: He laughs.

"What's so funny?" I say.

"My dad was right," he says. "He said you were probably just scamming us for the money. Well, you're not going to get away with it."

"I wasn't *scamming* you!" I'm outraged.

"Oh, no? Then where's the money?"

"They wouldn't give it back to me. When I said I wasn't going through with it, they said I couldn't have the money back."

Something about the way I speak the words must convince Tim that I'm telling the truth, because I see the dawning of reality come into his expression.

"Oh, no," he says quietly. "You're not really planning on . . . *having it*, are you?"

"That's exactly what I'm planning on," I say.

"But that's crazy, Angel," he says. "You can't do that."

"Yes," I say, "I can. And I plan to pay you and your

dad back every cent. I just can't yet. I still haven't told my parents."

"Then there's still time."

"Time for what?"

"Time to change your mind, of course."

"But I'm not going to change my mind."

"This is crazy talk. You're talking crazy. It doesn't have to be this way."

"Yes, it does. For me it does have to be this way."

He puts his face in his hands for a long moment. Then, finally, he looks up at me.

"What is it you want from me, Angel?"

His question surprises me, but even as I hear his words, I know there is only one answer:

"I don't want anything from you, Tim."

Week of December 17/Week 16

And I really don't want anything from Tim, which is exactly what I tell Karin as we sit in her bedroom.

We are supposed to be studying for our French IV final, but instead we are talking. Karin has been spending so much of her time with Todd lately, more and more as the days fly by, that it seems like forever since we last talked. In school, in the cafeteria, she mostly sits with Todd now, meaning she also sits with Danny Stanton and Ricky D'Amico. But we have studied together for every French test since freshman year, none of the people she now sits with at lunch even takes French, and so we are together again. It is the one subject besides English I have always scored higher in than Karin.

"How can you not want anything from him?" Karin asks.

"A better question would be, *Why* would I want anything from him?"

"Because this is all his fault?" she asks-answers. "Because if it weren't for him, you wouldn't be in this mess in the first place? Because, if you're going to go ahead with this . . . *insanity*—which I still don't completely understand—then it should be just as much his responsibility as yours?"

"And again," I say, "I come back to the same question: Why? Why would I want someone to be a part of this when that person so obviously does not want to be a part of it?"

"Because he should pay!"

I explain to Karin the same thing I explained to Tim: that I will pay him and his father back as soon as I tell my parents, that I do not want anything from either of them.

"But you should," she says.

"But I don't," I say.

I tell her what Tim's biggest concern was—that even if I pay him and his father back, once I begin to *show*, everyone will blame him for it, everyone will expect him to act like the father. I tell her what I told Tim, that this is the last thing on Earth I would ever want, that I will go to my grave before I ever tell anyone he is the father.

"But that's impossible!" she says. "Everyone will know!"

"No, it's not," I say. "The only way people will know for sure is if either you or Tim tell them. You're the only two people that I'm sure know about this. Hell, I'm not even sure his father knows my name. For all I know, Tim could have just referred to me as 'some girl from school' when he asked his father for the money."

"But everyone at school knows about you and him at Ricky D'Amico's party. People will talk."

"So let them talk. People will talk, but they won't *know* anything. I'll tell everyone, I'll tell my parents, it wasn't Tim. I'll tell them all it was someone else. I'll tell them all I won't say who it was."

"But he should be part of it," she says again.

"No," I say, "he shouldn't. His first instinct, upon hearing about it, was to tell me to get rid of it. I don't want him to be a part of any of this now."

For a while we leave Tim O'Mara behind and concentrate on studying for our French final. We drill each other on vocabulary lists, and I help Karin translate a long passage from a contemporary French novelist.

Karin has always been so much better than I am at most other subjects, she has always been such a big help, that rather than feeling superior I always just feel grateful to be able to help her with this one small thing.

Then something in the passage we are translating reminds her of Todd. Well, it seems that nearly everything reminds her of Todd these days.

"Have you ever noticed," she says, "how incredibly *cute* Todd looks when he eats french fries?"

I cannot honestly say that I have ever noticed this — Todd's incredible cuteness while eating french fries — but of course I cannot say this to Karin.

My best friend is obviously in love.

I can easily see this as she tells me about all of the other incredibly wonderful things that are embodied in the person of Todd. She tells me about everything she feels for him, everything they have done together.

For a while it feels like old times. It feels like the time that came Before.

Still, it is hard for me to hear Karin go on and on about Todd. Of course I am happy for her. What kind of best friend would I be if I weren't happy for her happiness? But every time she is talking about doing things with Todd, she is almost always talking about doing things with Danny Stanton and Ricky D'Amico as well—they are practically a regular foursome now—and I can't help but think *I* should be part of that equation. And then when Karin talks about the things she and Todd do alone together, even though it reminds me of the talks we used to have, it also all sounds so *normal*, it makes me realize how far apart our lives have grown, how far from normal my current life is.

Suddenly I realize I have my own special secret I want to share. I raise the hem of my shirt slightly with one hand, pull down the waistband of my jeans with the other. There is just the tiniest of bumps there now. If I didn't know what it was myself, I would think I was just someone who had eaten a larger dinner than normal and was just a little bit bloated, that it would pass in a few hours. But this will not pass. It will only get bigger.

"Do you want to touch it?" I ask shyly.

But Karin just stares, then shakes her head, as though horrified at the thought. "No, thanks," she says. It is clear she wants no part of this.

Then she flops down on her bed, rolls over on her back, studies the ceiling.

"I just don't get you, Angel," she says. "I don't get why you have to make this so hard on yourself and on everyone else."

And I can see, at last, that I am a puzzle to her. She is my very best friend in the whole wide world and I am a puzzle to her. But perhaps that is not so surprising because, these days, I am a puzzle even to myself.

Week of December 24/Week 17

Ever since Dr. Caldwell gave me the pregnancy book, I have taken to reading a little bit each night in bed before going to sleep. When I'm finished with my reading for the night, I put the book back in its hiding place: an old empty shoe box on the top shelf of my closet, putting a floppy hat over the box. The reading fascinates me in a way that is both exciting and horrifying at the same time: I read about the changes my body has undergone, has yet to undergo, I read about the options for delivery, I read about how the baby is changing too.

But as fascinating as the reading is, I have found myself being more and more tired lately, despite the book saying I should feel less tired now and despite the fact that I did for a while. And on the night before Christmas Eve, with my entire family due here the following night—everyone comes here each year for Christmas Eve *and* Christmas Day—I make a tragic error: I fall asleep with the book in my hands. This is the position I am in on Christmas Eve morning when my mother comes in to wake me so I can help her finish cleaning the house, start making the pies.

"Angel! *Angel!* Wake up!"

I feel her tugging on my arm, hear her anxious words even as I groggily swim up to consciousness.

"What the hell is that you're reading?"

Before I can even look at the book in my hands to see

what she's talking about, I can hear how serious this is: My mother almost never swears, has always said that swearing is something reserved for people who just aren't creative enough. "There is nothing creative about using 'fuck' as an all-purpose noun/verb/adverb," she always says. "Powerful language has more impact when used sparingly."

As I come fully awake, I recognize that this moment had to happen. Yet I have been avoiding it for so long, have only felt panic and fear any time I've let my mind light on it, certainly have not sought it out, as though believing that if I never said anything about it, perhaps no one else would ever notice.

But now that this moment is here, there is nothing else for it but to tell the truth.

"It's a guide to pregnancy, Mom," I say, feeling as tired as if I've never slept at all. "I'm pregnant."

My mom looks at me for a long time, anger and disbelief and sadness mixing on her face, then she picks up the phone on my desk, calls my dad.

Even though it is Christmas Eve day, he went into the office. He is such a workaholic that he always does this: goes in on Christmas Eve day and works until two or three, when he comes home to help with the preparations.

I hear my mom say, "I need you home here, Steve. *Now.*"

When he arrives home, looking like he raced the wind to get here, we are seated in the living room. I'm still in my pajamas and bathrobe on the couch, my feet tucked under me, while Mom sits in one of the side chairs, an untouched cup of coffee on the table before her. We have been sitting in silence like this since she made the call.

My dad sits down in the other side chair, jacket still on, leaning forward with hands clasped between his knees.

"So," he says, "what's up?"

This setup is so familiar. For as long as I can remember this has always been the position we assume whenever there is a need for a family conference. This is the position we sat in when I got in trouble in first grade for calling Billy Bailey a weenie, this is the position we sat in when Karin and I got in trouble freshman year for sneak-drinking during a dance, this is the position we sat in when I was eight years old and my mother had to tell me that I wasn't going to be getting a younger brother or sister after all.

But it has never felt like this.

"She's pregnant," my mom says, almost as though she is spitting out the words.

I can't help it. Just like even if you are trying to be a good person you can't help but look at a car wreck for at least a minute, in that minute of involuntary looking I see first shock on my dad's face and then an expression I've never seen before: disappointment. With all the things I have done wrong over the years, some minor and some major, while he hasn't always loved everything I've done, he's never looked at me like this.

I have never felt anything but loved by both my parents, but in this moment I can't help but feel that they love me a little less. And that is, so far, the hardest thing of all.

"How long?" my dad asks.

"Yes," my mother demands, "how long?"—a question she didn't ask before.

"About four months," I say.

"Four—" My mother nearly leaps out of her chair.

"When were you planning on telling us? Or *were* you even planning on telling us? What were you planning to do, be like one of those girls who has the baby in secret and throws it in the Dumpster?"

We have all read the stories about those girls, the stories that make us wonder, incredulously, "What could she have been thinking?" "And how could no one have noticed?"

In a way, I understand those girls now, at least in part, understand being so confused and scared you become like a deer in the headlights, unable to do anything to prevent your own disaster, hoping that something else will come along to save you because you can't act for yourself. But I still can't understand the Dumpster thing.

"God, no!" I say.

"Then what was your plan?" my mother demands again.

"I don't know!" I say. "I didn't have *a plan*!"

"Clearly," my dad mutters.

"So," my mom says, tapping her foot, "you didn't have a plan before. Well, then, what are you planning to do now?"

"I'm having the baby," I say.

"What?" she almost shrieks. "And then what," she says, "put it up for adoption?"

"No," I say, and in that one word I hear the truth of what I have decided without even realizing that I had decided it. If I'm going to have this baby, I can no more give it away for adoption than I can throw it in a Dumpster. I have already paid too much, come too far. "I'm going to keep it."

"And how do you plan on raising it?" my mom says. "What about school?"

"I haven't gotten that far yet," I say.

"It's not too late," my mom says. "Sure, you've passed the first trimester, but there's still time. You could still get an abortion."

"I could make some calls," my dad says, starting to rise from his seat.

"No!" I shout. "I'm going to keep this baby . . . with or without your help."

"Who's the father?" my dad demands. "Who did this to you?"

But I tell myself that I will never answer that question. I don't want them to know.

"Was it Danny?" my mother asks. "You used to spend a lot of time with Danny."

"No," I say, "definitely not Danny."

"Who, then?" my dad asks.

But still I won't answer that.

And so it goes, with my parents trying to get more information out of me, with my parents trying to alter the course I have set myself upon.

Week of December 31/Week 18

I spent Christmas, both eve and day, in my bedroom. It was something my parents and I mutually agreed on without spelling it out.

"You're probably a little tired," my mom said.

"You probably have a lot to think about," my dad said.

Both of which were true.

And yet I knew that a big part of why they were suggesting this was because they couldn't face the idea of seeing me at the holiday table, knowing what they now know.

"We're not going to say anything to anyone else about this," my mom said.

129

"Of course not," my dad said.

And I could tell they were both still hoping I'd change my mind. Or that they could change it for me.

So I spent the holiday in my bedroom, my mom and dad bringing up trays for me. Through the walls I could hear it when my mother told each arriving visitor I wouldn't be joining them this year, saying that I had the flu, could hear the concern of the others, could hear it when my next-oldest cousin said grace over the meal.

At one point my grandmother knocked on my door on her way to the bathroom.

"What is it, Angel?" she said, sitting down on the bed beside me, placing her cool hand on my forehead. "You don't feel warm to me. Is there something else going on that your parents aren't telling us about?"

I looked at her dyed champagne hair, the crinkle around those dark eyes I knew so well.

"No, Grandmother," I said, hoping to put away her fears while at the same time hoping she wouldn't push with any more questions. "I overdid it studying for finals this year. I think I just need to sleep some more."

After she left me to go back downstairs, I tried to tell myself the reason my parents suggested I spend the holiday in my room wasn't that they were ashamed of me.

And I continued to tell myself that as the next week of vacation wore on.

They never said I couldn't leave the house, never said I was grounded, and yet I remained in the house all the same. It is like I can hear them waiting, hear the very walls of the house waiting, to hear what will come next.

Finally, on New Year's Eve, I can't take it anymore.

"Where are you going?" my mom asks when she sees me come downstairs with my coat on.

"Out," I say.

"Yes, but where? Are you going to a party?"

Even though Karin invited me to go to Ricky D'Amico's New Year's Eve party with her, I said no.

"No," I say, "I just need to get out for a while."

"What time will you be back?" my dad asks.

"I'm not sure," I say. "Later on sometime."

"Hey," he says, "we'd like some answers here. You can't just go out till all hours and not tell us where you're going or when you'll be back."

"What are you worried about," I say, "that I'll get pregnant? It's not like I can still get pregnant."

Before I slam the door behind me, I can see on their faces that this is the cruelest thing I've ever said to them.

january

WE ARE JUST SITTING DOWN TO DINNER—STEAK, WHICH
I can't even stand the name of now, let alone the smell,
and cheesy potatoes, which suddenly sounds like the
greatest food ever invented—when the doorbell rings.

It is Tim O'Mara and his father.

"Daniel. What are you doing here?" my dad asks
Tim's dad.

I have forgotten that Daniel O'Mara is a lawyer too,
that Tim's dad and my dad know each other through
work.

Daniel O'Mara is an older version of Tim, that sandy
blond hair thinning on top and less curly, his brown
eyes tired, his belly turning a bit to paunch.

"May we come in?" Mr. O'Mara asks formally.

"Of course," Dad says.

My mother says hello, asks if she can get them

133

something to drink as everyone sits down in the living room, as dinner grows cold on the table.

"Thanks," says Mr. O'Mara, "but this isn't a social visit. We're here to talk about . . . her." He gives me only the briefest of glances before looking off into the corner. "And about the . . . baby."

"You know about . . . ?" My mother starts in her seat.

It turns out that Tim has been doing what I was doing for so long: avoiding the truth. His dad must have been pressuring him about the receipt, Tim must have kept putting him off, only to have to finally admit there wasn't going to be one, that the girl he'd gotten pregnant had decided not to have an abortion after all.

I guess that at first Tim refused to tell him who the girl was, but Tim's father finally pressured him into telling him that as well.

And now they are here.

I think I maybe know what Tim's father wants, but I am not sure.

"I understand that these things can be very delicate," Mr. O'Mara says cautiously, "but, surely, you must all see the . . . idiocy of going through with this thing." He speaks directly to my dad, as though the rest of us aren't even there, as though this is something to be decided between the two men. "It's not too late for us to turn this thing around, Steve. There are doctors who would—"

"But that's not what Angel wants," my dad says, and I hear an anger in his voice unlike anything I have ever heard before. After everything we've been through in the last several days here, after all the silent disappointment, I am shocked to hear my dad standing up for me. "It's Angel's choice," my dad tells Mr. O'Mara, "and this is what she chooses to do."

"Angel's not the only person involved here, Steve," Mr. O'Mara says evenly. "It's not that simple."

"You're right about that," my dad agrees. "*Your son* got my daughter into this mess. *Your son* should pay for what he's done."

I can see Mr. O'Mara mulling this over. I can see that this is not how he expected this to go at all. He probably thought he could persuade us, persuade *me*, to see his version of reason. But before his very eyes his plans for the way things should be are falling apart.

"I can see where you would feel that way," Mr. O'Mara at last admits, grudgingly. "And, of course, if Angel insists on going through with this . . . *thing*, we'll need to contribute something financially. We can work that out. And, of course, Tim's mother will need to be told. She'll be angry at first, of course, but eventually she'll come around. She'll probably even decide she likes the idea of having a grandchild. I just don't want to see Tim's chances in life destroyed by this. Surely you can understand that?"

From the expression on my dad's face, my mom's face, I can see that, even though they are still very mad at both Tim and Mr. O'Mara, they are pleased that Mr. O'Mara is starting to see things reasonably. They are nodding their heads in approval, even if maybe they don't like every single one of his word choices.

At last I find my voice.

"No!" I say.

Everyone turns to me.

"No!" I say. "To everything!"

My dad is clearly puzzled.

"Angel?" he says.

I look at my parents. I am talking straight to them. Frankly, I don't care what Tim and his father think.

"When I first told Tim about this, do you know what

his first reaction was?" I say. "He wanted me to kill it. Do you think I would want someone like *that* involved in my baby's life?" I go on, talking about Mr. O'Mara as if he weren't even there, "And Mr. O'Mara. Do you know what he said when Tim asked him for money for the abortion? He said he wanted Tim to bring him *a receipt*. It wasn't enough what had happened, what I was going through, he needed *proof* his money was being well spent. Do you think I'd want someone like *that* involved in my baby's life now?"

My dad turns to Mr. O'Mara, disbelief, horror, anger on his face.

"What kind of a person *are* you?" he says.

"I'm just a father, like you, Steve," he says. "I want the right thing for my son, just like you want for Angel."

"Get out," my dad says.

"Look," says Mr. O'Mara, "if you're not going to let us be a part of the baby's life, I don't want this thing hanging over Tim's head forever. I don't want everyone talking about him, saying whatever, that he's not taking responsibility or whatever."

"I never wanted anyone to know it was Tim in the first place," I say. "I certainly won't say anything. Ever."

"We'll draw up the papers next week," my dad says. "We'll renounce all claim of support."

"How will Angel take care of the baby by herself?" Mr. O'Mara asks.

"Her father and I will help her," my mother says.

I know that even a half hour ago my mother was totally against this. But I can see that she is so offended by Mr. O'Mara—maybe she would even say now that she is *fucking* offended by him—that she will not stand down from his challenge. It would be nice if she were supporting me because she actually believed in and supported my decision, but I know she is doing this out of anger toward someone else: Mr. O'Mara. Still, for now, I will take what I can get. It's all I have.

"We'll renounce all claim of support," my dad says again, "and you'll sign papers saying you give up all rights to being part of the baby's life. Now *get out*."

Week of January 14/Week 20

I go see Dr. Caldwell for my next visit.

She wants to know how I've been feeling, what's been going on in my life.

138

I tell her I've been feeling great, which is true—once again the constant feeling of tiredness is gone and I no longer feel as nauseous as I did in the first few months—and I tell her that lately I have this superhuman kind of energy that makes me feel like I could do just about anything.

"Well, enjoy that superhuman kind of energy while it lasts," she says, and laughs. "And don't try to lift anything big like a car, even if it feels like you could."

She looks at my chart to see what the nurse has written down on it.

"Your blood pressure is up quite a bit from last time," she says. "I'm not loving that. Tell me what else is going on with you."

I tell her what should be my big news. "School acceptances came in the mail," I say. "I got into Yale."

"That's terrific news!" she says.

"I'm not going, of course," I say.

When I told Robin Keating that, he was nearly livid.

"You got into the only school you were interested in applying to, and now you're not going?" he said.

I told him what I am telling Dr. Caldwell now.

"I decided to go to the community college instead," I say.

What I didn't go on to explain to Robin, but what Dr. Caldwell clearly understands, is that Yale would have been too far. If I am going to have this baby, then until I can afford to pay for a daytime babysitter myself, I will have to go to a school where I can live at home, so my mother can help with the baby during the daytime.

Despite what my mother said to Mr. O'Mara, about her and my father intending to help me out, she was less supportive after he left.

"What am I supposed to do," she said, "give up my accounting practice so I can raise your baby?"

"It'll all work out, Hel," my dad said. "So maybe you'll need to rearrange your schedule sometimes."

"Why is it *my* life that has to change?" my mother said. "I didn't ask for this. I already had *my* baby. I figured the next time I spent a lot of time with a baby, sure, it would be my grandchild, but that grandchild would be coming here to visit occasionally, not to *live* here."

"So my life'll change too," my dad said. "When you need me to, I'll rearrange my schedule too. I'll help."

"You could still change your mind," my mom said to

me, despite what she'd said to Mr. O'Mara. "It's still not too late."

But for me it is too late.

"Don't worry," my dad said, after my mom stormed out of the room. "Somehow it'll be all right."

But things are not all right, certainly not between them. At night I often hear them fighting. I know it is about me.

"So what's so great about Yale, anyway?" Dr. Caldwell shrugs now, and with that one shrug erases the last wisp of smoke from an entire dream. "If a person with a C average from Yale can go on to become president of the United States, it seems to me that an A average somewhere else could probably get you pretty far too. You'll just have to be brilliant somewhere else."

One thing I do not tell Dr. Caldwell is about the rumors. If people whispered a lot back in the fall about me going off with Tim O'Mara the night of Ricky D'Amico's party, now that hum that follows me around school is beginning to turn into a roar.

I am still not totally showing yet, just a slight thickening around the middle, but I can hear kids at school speculating.

"What's up with Angel?"

"Do you think she needs an eating disorder?"

Sometimes I try to tell myself I'm just imagining the whispers. Sometimes I tell myself it doesn't matter if people think I'm gaining weight because I'm depressed or for whatever reason, that it doesn't matter what anyone thinks.

"Are you ready for that ultrasound now?" Dr. Caldwell asks.

I have been nervous about this, even though I know from reading the book she gave me that an ultrasound doesn't hurt at all. But what if the ultrasound shows that there is something terribly wrong with the baby, something awful that can't be fixed? I have already decided on my own that if this is the case, I will not go through with the pregnancy, even as a part of me feels guilty at my reaction, wondering if I would still be relieved at such an outcome. Still, I feel more and more all the time that I know what I am capable of. And I know that if there is something terribly wrong with this baby, I won't be able to go through with this.

The book Dr. Caldwell gave me was right: The ultrasound doesn't hurt at all, but it does give me the inside squirmies when she squirts the clear blue gel onto my slightly swollen belly and uses this wand thing to move it around so she can see on the monitor what is going on inside me.

"Toes, fingers, heart," she says, eyes on the screen. "Everything is exactly where it's supposed to be. Do you want to look?"

So far I have been studiously staring at the ceiling, worried about seeing something scary on the screen. Now I turn my head to the right so I can see what she is seeing.

To me it looks like a picture of another galaxy. There is a darkish background, with swirling mists of stars on it. At first I do not make out any of the details and I think that whatever Dr. Caldwell is seeing, it must be different from what I am seeing.

All I know is that this is the first time I have seen what is growing inside me and, in its own otherworldly kind of way, it's beautiful.

"See this?" Dr. Caldwell traces her finger on the screen. "There's the baby's head. And this slight indent here? That's the baby's mouth."

And now I can clearly see what she is pointing to: My baby has a head. It has a mouth.

143

"Do you want to know what sex the baby is going to be?" she asks.

"You can tell that just from looking at that picture?" I say.

"I can make a pretty good guess," she says. "I could always be wrong, but it looks pretty certain."

"That's okay," I say. "Let it be a surprise to look forward to. Besides, I have my own pretty good guess about whether this is a boy or a girl."

I don't want to hear her pretty good guess, and I don't want to make mine, not out loud. What if our guesses don't agree? Or what if one of us is wrong or our guesses agree and we're both wrong? I do not want to get my mind wrapped around a certain outcome, only to have it turn out differently.

After I get dressed, Dr. Caldwell says she'd like to talk to me for a few more minutes.

She tells me that before long it'll be March, that the baby's due just three months after that, so I'll need to start thinking about signing up for Lamaze classes, if that's the way I want to go, and that I also need to start thinking about taking breast-feeding classes.

"Again," she says, "if that's the way you want to go."

144

"They have classes for that?"

"You'd be surprised"—she laughs—"at how much harder certain perfectly natural things are than you think they'd be."

Huh.

"I'm still a little worried about that elevated blood pressure," she says. "I'm also slightly concerned that you haven't gained quite as much weight as women usually do at this point."

"Aren't most people too heavy in this country anyway?" I say.

"Perhaps," she says, "but pregnancy is no time for strict dieting."

"I haven't been dieting," I insist.

"That's good, then," she says. Then she repeats something I have already read in the book. "You know," she says, "a lot of women go along and go along not really showing at all, and then one day—*pop!*—that belly is right out there."

I'm about to go when she stops me.

"Hey, I almost forgot," she says, waving what looks like two photographs in her hands. "Do you want these?"

They are printed-out pictures from the ultrasound with the name HANSEN, ANGEL printed in one corner, the date and time stamped underneath.

I take them, look at that swirling galaxy again, the shape of that head, the tiny indented mouth.

"Yes," I say, unable to tear my eyes away. The deeper I get into this thing, despite the constant underlying fears, I grow more certain all the time. "I do want them."

Week of January 21/Week 21

Dr. Caldwell obviously knows what she is talking about, because what she described is exactly what happens to me. I have just been going along and going along, letting people speculate that maybe I've just put on a little extra weight for whatever reason, when one day—*pop!*—my belly sticks out, my former innie belly button now turned into an outie, and there is no mistaking the fact that I am pregnant.

"That's *it*," my mother says when I come down to breakfast one morning, wearing a pair of my dad's jeans rolled up at the ankles, because at last none of mine fit anymore, one of his red and navy rep ties woven through the belt loops because if my pants are too tight, his are still too loose. Over this I have one of my gauze shirts left over from summer. Even though it is very cold out now, and we are finally getting the kind of severely frigid New England winter my mother always talks about from her youth, the free-flowing material is the only thing in my closet that will cover most of my belly without looking tight.

I'm not sure what my mother is getting at. Certainly *I* think the red and navy tie looks cool like that.

"I may not love what you're doing," my mom says, hands on hips, "but no daughter of *mine* is going to go around looking like a ragamuffin." Then she speaks words I never thought I'd hear her say: "You're skip-ping school today. We're going shopping."

When we get to the mall, we go straight to the mater-nity shop, Mommy Heaven, the window of which I'd gazed into back in October. Now that the high energy of making this decision to play hooky has worn off, my mom is all grim determination as she goes through the racks of clothes. She is a woman with a mission, but, obviously, it is not a pleasant mission.

"You'll need some jeans for now," she says, picking

out a few pairs with expandable waistbands, "but you'll also need some lighter things in bigger sizes for the late spring."

I submit to everything, letting her pile clothes up in my arms as she moves through the store.

Then she spots an outfit nailed to the wall that is not so very different from what I am wearing, except that the pieces aren't something hastily thrown together. Instead they are artfully designed to allow a woman to look pregnant without looking stupid, without looking like she threw out her fashion sense with her last pack of tampons; and, of course, the ankles of the jeans are much wider than those on my dad's jeans, much more like what you see women walking around in every day.

"We never had anything like that when I was pregnant with you," she says, her voice mixing pleasure with resentment. "Well," she adds, "we did have bell-bottoms when I was a teen, but pregnant women didn't get to wear them."

Her words remind me of how she always likes to point out that even though what she calls "your generation" likes to think they invented certain fashions, kids wore things that were very similar twenty-five years ago. There had been a few decades' worth of fashion changes and evolution in between, but we were basically back to the same stuff she and her friends wore.

"Well," she'll say, "except for those ridiculously loose pants guys wear these days. They're just *dumb*. But," she'll add, "I sure do wish I'd kept all my Candies and platform shoes, especially the ones with the four-inch cork heels."

It is hard to think that everything you believe you and your friends are inventing now was invented by your parents, lived through by them long before.

And it is also strange to think that maybe my mom and I are not so different after all. She loved cork heels. I love cork heels.

"Oh, what the heck," she says, asking the salesgirl to get the outfit that kind of looks like what I am already wearing, only better, down off the wall. "If you're going to dress like that, it might as well fit properly."

"Thanks," I say.

It has been a long time since we picked out clothes together. Usually, in the past couple of years before all this started, I would just ask my parents what the spending limit was and stand impatiently, enduring it while my mother reminded me yet again not to come home with any shirts that looked like bras. I can see now, from the brief smile that comes over my mother's face, that she has missed this: the simple pleasure of making clothing decisions together.

As we are leaving the store a while later, each carrying two shopping bags, I turn to my mom.

"Are you sorry you had me?" I ask, a question that has been bothering me, aware as I am now of what a disappointment I have been to her.

"God, Angel, what a question! Of course I'm not sorry I had you. I've never been sorry once, not since the first day I learned I was pregnant with you."

And I think that in this, for the most part, we are also not so very different from each other at all.

Week of January 28/Week 22

I have become the great Untouchable, the stupid girl who isn't smart enough to get an abortion.

At last Robin Keating understands my decision about not going to Yale.

"So," he sighs when I meet with him, "community college."

"It won't be so bad," I say to him, as though he is the one who needs reassurance. "And, anyway, I've been giving this a lot of thought."

"And?"

"What I want most is to be a writer, and I don't really think someone can teach you how to do that."

"Tell that to all the MFAs out there," he snorts.

MFA is a term I am only passingly familiar with, but I know what I'm trying to say here. I've thought about it a lot.

"I think you can become a writer through being a great reader, through reading widely, but I really don't think it can be taught. At best you might learn school-room techniques for making transition sentences or stuff like that, and you might learn what your teachers think a writer should be, but no one can teach you your own voice. You either have one, or maybe you find one, but no one can give that to you."

"Huh," he says. Then: "So why bother with college at all?"

"I guess I just figure that while I'm working on my

voice, I might as well pick up some useful skills, in case the voice I do find isn't good enough."

"You know," he says, and sighs, and I can see he can't stop himself from saying what he says next, even if it is unprofessional. "This could have all been so much easier for you."

And, of course, he's right. Certainly it's what everyone else thinks.

It's not as though I'm the first pregnant teen in the history of the world. I'm not even the first pregnant teen in the history of our school. But it seems that every other girl who has walked these halls before me, if she got pregnant, she either (1) had an abortion or (2) went ahead with the pregnancy only if she had no future anyone else would think of as worthwhile or if she had parental pressure to go through with it for religious reasons. It feels, sometimes, as though I am the only girl with a solid future who has chosen differently.

There is only one group of kids among whom my decision is popular: I have unwittingly and unwillingly become the poster girl for Students 4 Life.

"We think it's so cool you're going through with having your baby," says Kelly Bergstrom in the cafeteria.

"It's, like, maybe the coolest thing anyone in our class has ever done," says John Paul Johnson, his eyes bright.

Back in freshman year Kelly and John Paul founded Students 4 Life. It is an organization for determined virgins who promote an anti-abortion agenda. All of them have signed contracts with their parents, saying they will not have sex before marriage. They have even been known to publicly shun classmates they suspect of having abortions.

"Well," John Paul adds, "of course it would have been even cooler if you'd waited until you were married."

No matter how many times I try to tell them, they do not understand that their political agenda means nothing to me, that this is not about that.

Finally, frustrated, I brush them off.

"Please call us if you ever need support in what you're doing," Kelly calls after me.

Over my dead body, I think, recognizing the unkindness of my thought while at the same time not caring about that unkindness at all.

Whatever this journey I am on is, it is not their journey.

I ask Karin if she will go to the basketball game with me, and she asks if it is okay if we just meet up there, that she told Todd she would drive over with him. I do not know why I even want to go to the game so much—it is not as though I am such a huge fan of basketball, after all, in and of itself—and it is not as though Danny and I have talked at all lately, Danny being the only reason I ever started going to basketball games in the first place. Still, there is something so reassuring about watching Danny Stanton's easy stride as he runs down the court, as I sit in the stands by myself, having been unable to spot Karin as yet. There is something so familiar about watching Danny Stanton use his hand to brush his hair, slightly damp with sweat, off his forehead, watching him jump, watching him shoot, watching him score.

It is as though he somehow lives in a place I used to be a part of.

At halftime I notice something I haven't noticed before: Seated not even a half dozen seats away from me is Tim O'Mara.

Since our return from winter break, since I have started to show, I have noticed a change. The buzz that used to follow me around last September, after Ricky

D'Amico's party, now follows Tim, and he no longer looks cocky or sure. Instead he looks down or away whenever I pass him in the hall. And for the first time, sitting there in the stands, it occurs to me what is happening: People have done the math, they have figured the distance between September and now, and they have concluded Tim must be the father of my baby.

I look over at him and realize that he is going through what I went through: the feeling, not quite paranoid because what you suspect is true, that everyone is talking about you.

A part of me is briefly glad this is happening to Tim. I had to go through this, so why shouldn't he? After all, if he hadn't started rumors about me in the first place, this wouldn't be happening to him now.

But another part of me hates this, hates the idea of anyone still linking me with Tim O'Mara in their minds.

I scan the crowd until at last I find Karin, sitting next to Todd. I climb over the bleachers, awkwardly, huffing and puffing by the time I collapse on the bench near her side.

"What's wrong?" she asks.

"Make it stop," I say.

"Huh?"

"I don't care what you do. Make up a rumor," I say, realizing even as I say it that I'm letting Tim off the hook but not caring at all about that. "Tell people it was some guy nobody here knows, from some other school. Just make it stop."

february

I STUDY THE MENU AT THE DINER AS THOUGH IT IS SOME-thing important, finally settling on a grilled cheese sandwich with a side salad. I really have a craving for tuna fish, but the book Dr. Caldwell gave me says tuna fish is an item to be avoided while pregnant.

"I'll have the same," Aunt Stacey says to the waitress. Then she smiles at me. "It's been a long time since I had a grilled cheese sandwich."

Aunt Stacey is my mom's older sister by five years. If Mom is the prettiest one in the family, then Aunt Stacey has always been the coolest. She wears her own dark hair in a short spiky cut I only wish I could look good in, wears clothes that don't look much different from Karin's. She's a psychologist with two college-age kids and one divorce to her credit, and she has asked me to have lunch here with her today for I know not what reason.

"How have you been feeling?" she asks, as the waitress sets our sandwiches down. "Is everything going okay with the pregnancy?"

I don't answer at first because my mouth is full with the first bite of sandwich, which tastes like bliss, all melted cheese and soft buttered toast.

Now that I am well into my second trimester, the nausea is gone and it is incredible how much I enjoy eating. At first it was hard to give myself permission to eat whenever I was hungry. After all, I am an American girl living in the early years of the twenty-first century, meaning that I have been flirting with eating disorders all my life. But I know it is important for the baby to get proper nutrition, and so I allow myself to eat whenever I am hungry, without overeating, avoiding the foods Dr. Caldwell's book says I should avoid. Still, it is amazing how good simple food tastes when you are not worrying every second about every calorie and what it'll do to your body.

"Great," I say at last. "I'm feeling great. Everything's going fine."

"I know it hasn't been easy with your parents," she says. "Helena does seem to be having a hard time accepting that this is what you choose to do."

Even though I know that Aunt Stacey and Mom talk a lot to each other—they are sisters, after all, and close—it is still a vague shock to think that when they are talking, sometimes they are talking about *me*.

"It's okay," I say. "I mean, I'm not sure I really expected anything different."

Aunt Stacey puts her sandwich down, studies me for a long enough minute that I start to get uncomfortable. Do I have gooey cheese stuck to my chin?

"*I* was pregnant once," she says at last.

"Actually, Aunt Stacey," I say, laughing, "you were pregnant twice. Remember?"

"I'm not talking about Kim and Karl," she says, naming her kids.

I stop eating.

"I mean before I had them," she says.

"What?" is the smartest thing I can think to say.

"When I was in high school," she says, "I got pregnant. Like you."

I feel my mouth drop open as if to say something, but no words come out.

"Well, not exactly like you," Aunt Stacey amends. "I was just fifteen at the time."

I close my mouth.

"Don't you want to know what happened?" Aunt Stacey asks.

I nod.

"I had an abortion," she says.

As shocking as what she already told me was, about being pregnant when she was even younger than I am now, this is more shocking yet. How peculiar it is to have someone be a part of your life for so long—my aunt has known me since before I was born, helped my mom get through the first stages of having a new baby in the house, has always been really like a second mom to me—and realize that you do not really know that other person at all.

"Does my mom know?" is all I can think to ask.

Aunt Stacey surprises me by laughing. "God, no!" she says. "And don't you tell her either."

"Why are you telling me, then?" I ask. "And why wouldn't you want Mom to know?"

"To answer your first question, I'm not really sure. Maybe I just wanted you to know you're not the first person in this family that this has ever happened to. As for your second, Helena has always been so sure of exactly what she wanted—she never slept with anyone before your father, and then they totally planned on having you—that I guess I always just figured if she knew, she would judge me in some way."

I'm not so sure about that. They are sisters, after all. But then I figure, it's Aunt Stacey's story to tell, to whomever she wants. Or not.

"What happened?" I ask, suddenly really wanting to know.

"I was young," she says, "and stupid. No more stupid than most"—she shrugs—"but stupid enough."

"For having the abortion?" I ask.

"No," she says, "for getting pregnant in the first place. The guy who got me that way was certainly no one I really cared about. That was the stupid part."

"But what about the abortion?" I really want to know this. "Don't you ever regret the abortion?"

Aunt Stacey gives this more thought than anything I've said before.

"You know," she says, "of course I've wondered at times about what it would have been like. I've done the math and figured out how old the baby would have been at different times in my life. And I guess it's always only natural to wonder about what the lives we're not living must be like. I mean, don't you wonder sometimes about what your life would be like right now if you *hadn't* decided to keep the baby?"

I nod. Of course I've wondered that. Certainly, things would be simpler. At least in some ways.

"But, no." She shakes her head. "I can't honestly say that I've ever regretted it. I felt that I was doing the right thing for me at the time, and I just couldn't see any other choice, being who I was." She laughs. "Maybe I'm more like Helena than I like to think. We both set our sights on something and hold on tight. I wanted to go to college, I wanted to become a psychologist from the time I was twelve, and I couldn't see how I could do all that if I had a baby at fifteen, and definitely not with a guy I didn't even really care about."

I sit and I think about what she has been saying, about my mother and her and me and how it all somehow ties together in a single tapestry of fabric, and I begin to get a glimmering of an idea. It is so easy for people to look at someone else and think, "I would never do that" or "I would never let myself get in that situation" or "I would never make the choices you've made." It's a lot harder to simply sit and listen and allow other people the space to be who they are. Why do we have to judge people for not being us? Why do we feel judged by other people for not being them?

"Okay," Aunt Stacey says, as though she can read my thoughts, "this is getting *way* too serious. Before, I said I wasn't sure what I wanted to talk to you about today or why I told you what I told you, and now I think it's simply this:"—she puts her hand over mine, holds on to my fingers tightly—"I think you're going to be *fine*, Angel. And you and Helena are eventually going to be just *fine* together. We all do what we need to do, given who we are."

Week of February 11/Week 24

"That's a pretty top," my mom says when I come downstairs. I hear the sound of my dad in the kitchen, singing some old Rolling Stones song while doing the dinner dishes. "Where are you going?"

She's right, it is a pretty top, dark red velvet with matching satin ribbon under the breast area, the sleeves belling outward. I went shopping for it myself after

163

school yesterday, and I wear it now over one of my pairs of expandable-waist jeans. I have even put on some makeup for this occasion, the first I've put on in a long time.

"I'm going to the Valentine's Day dance at school," I tell her.

"Do you have a date?" she asks, surprised.

I laugh at the very idea.

"No," I say. "I'm going stag, or whatever the word for it is when a girl goes alone."

"But . . . *why*?" she says.

"Oh, come on," I say, "what about all those times I've gone to dances with Karin? I don't need a date to go to a dance."

"So you're going with Karin, then," she says, relieved.

"No," I say patiently. "I just told you, I'm going by myself."

She shakes her head. "I honestly don't understand you, Angel," she says, and it's clear she doesn't. "I don't know why you need to make everything harder on yourself than it is already."

"Look, I'm tired, Mom. Okay? I'm tired of feeling like I've done something wrong, like I'm abnormal in some way. I just want to be able to do what everyone else does again. If *this*"—I indicate my belly—"hadn't happened, I'd be going to this dance. If no one asked me, I'd be going with Karin. If Karin weren't available, I'd go by myself, just so I could be a part of what everyone else is a part of. There are bound to be other girls there who don't have dates; I'll just hook up with some of them. Why should I let *this* stop me?"

It's clear my mother doesn't have an answer to this, which is good, because I intend to do what I set out to do. I don't want to wait on the sidelines anymore for life to find me again. I'm a high school girl—okay, a *pregnant* high school girl—and I just want to have the experiences everyone else is having. I want what is coming to me.

"Well, drive carefully," my mom says, "and don't be too late."

But of course I am not like everybody else, and that knowledge hits me in the face just as soon as I walk into the dance, the cafeteria hung with pink and red decorations. I am like no one else at all.

If I had thought about it ahead of time, I would have realized that Ricky D'Amico would be at her usual early-evening post, taking tickets at the door. But I hadn't given any thought to that ahead of time. And if I'd given any thought to Ricky being at the door, I would have realized that Danny would be there right beside her.

Danny Stanton has now been going out with Ricky D'Amico for a longer period of time than I can remember him ever going out with anybody else. There have been many times when I have wondered, *What does he see in her?*

But as I walk up to the table, as I see her sitting there with her auburn hair swept back in a rhinestone clasp, the imitation so real it almost looks like diamonds, wearing a pink silk slip of a dress that looks more like something you'd wear to bed with someone you were really into than something you'd wear to a dance, I have to admit the truth. Ricky D'Amico, whatever else she is, is a stunningly pretty girl.

Danny, as usual, turns away from me when he sees me coming, but Ricky has no problem looking at me head-on.

"Well," she says, "just look what Mother, um, *Nature* dragged in." Then she recites her next words so perfectly, one hand to her cheek in mock horror, that a part of me wonders if she's practiced this, waiting for just such an occasion: "Old Angel Hansen lived in a shoe, she was about to have a baby, oh, what would she do?"

Danny may not be looking, but he is certainly listening, because he turns to Ricky sharply, anger all over his face.

"*What* did you just say to her?" he says.

I don't hear how Ricky responds, because I am already turning away from them, moving quickly for the door. Whatever else goes on between them, I don't hear it, only hear her shouting, *"Danny!"*

As I run out of the cafeteria, I hear Danny shout after me, *"Angel!"* It is the first word he has spoken to me in I can't even say how long, but I don't stop running. I run out the doors of the school, run to my car, and it is not until I'm fumbling with the key in the lock that I realize it started to snow while I was inside.

The flakes are big, downy, soft, but I don't care about that, don't care about anything as I key the ignition, turn on the radio as loud as it will go. *I need to drown the words of Ricky D'Amico*, I think, *need to drown the sound of her taunting me*.

I am pulling out of the driveway, feeling the bass

guitar thrumming through the car, feeling as though it is thrumming right through my body, erasing everything, when I hear, over the sound of the music, the noise of a car horn blaring and the screech of the tires of a car failing to brake in time, as a car plows into me from the left.

After that, I remember nothing.

Week of February 18/Week 25

When I wake up in the hospital, my mom is seated in a chair holding my hand, my dad standing behind her with his hand on her shoulder.

I start to rise in the bed.

"Is the baby okay?" I say. "Is she okay?"

"She?" my mom says.

I have never said that aloud before, that I am convinced the baby will be a girl.

"She or he is fine," my dad says.

"It was touch and go there for a while," my mom says, "but now it seems like everything is going to be fine."

I settle back into the pillows, ask what happened.

"You were pulling out of the school parking lot," my dad says, "and some *jerk* ran a red light and smashed right into you."

"You were unconscious when they brought you in," my mom says. "Your left ankle is sprained and you were hit pretty hard in the head when you struck the windshield. There was blood all over the place."

I reach my hand to my forehead, feel the bandage beneath my hairline there.

"You have a concussion and you lost a lot of blood," my dad says. "Head injuries are always the worst."

"Why weren't you wearing your seat belt?" my mother asks.

I shake my head like I don't remember.

"Why did you leave the dance so early?" my dad asks.

I shake my head again. I don't want to say it was because I was so upset, I don't want to say I didn't put on my seat belt because I just wasn't thinking straight at the time.

"But the baby—," I start to ask again.

"Is fine," my mother says. "Dr. Caldwell was very concerned at first—all that blood you lost—but then

169

things turned for the better and she said we'd be surprised how resilient babies are."

I smile because that sounds exactly like Dr. Caldwell. She is always saying that.

Up until the moment of the accident, up until *now*, there have still been times when I thought that maybe it wouldn't be such a bad thing if some kind of accident *did* happen to me, some kind of accident that wasn't my fault but that would resolve the issue of the baby all the same. Maybe I would then be able to go back to the life I was leading before, get back on the track I had previously set for myself.

Did I purposely pull out into the street, in the hopes of getting hit?

No, I realize. Nothing I was thinking about on the night of the Valentine's Day dance was that deliberate. I quite simply wasn't thinking at all, my entire impulse being to get way from Ricky D'Amico as fast as I could.

Before, I would have said I was only having this baby because I could see no other choice for myself, being me, to make. I would have said, if I was being honest, that I was only doing it because I felt like I *had* to do it, because I would have felt too guilty not to.

But now I see something I never saw before: I *want* this baby. Maybe I didn't before, not really, maybe I was just doing things out of some extreme sense of responsibility. But I want it now.

"The baby is fine," my mom says again, "and you're going to be fine too."

"We love you," my dad says. "Everything's going to be just fine."

Week of February 25/Week 26

I am still at home nursing my injured ankle. Even though the doctors gave me this crutch to help me get around, which I should only need hopefully for another week, my parents are worried that if I go to school, I will slip on the ice. Ever since Valentine's Day we have gotten at least three more snowfalls, as though the heavens decided we needed to make up for the relatively mild winter of the year before, and late into my sixth month of pregnancy it is hard enough to get my unfamiliar bulk around, let alone trying to negotiate a crutch and ice as well.

My father is at work, of course, and my mother has

gone off to do the grocery shopping, as I sit on the couch in the living room, still in my bathrobe even though it is late afternoon, watching TV. But neither soap operas nor talk shows interest me, and the early reports of spring break on MTV only serve to depress me. It is impossible to think I will ever want to put on a bathing suit in public again, let alone a bikini with a thong bottom. So I am staring out the big picture window, lamenting the growing size of my butt as I take in the view of six inches of unsullied white snow on the lawn, when I see Danny Stanton walk by the window, a winter coat shielding his body, something green and cone-shaped held in his hand. As much as I would like to change into something less . . . frumpy-looking, he is at the door ringing the bell before I can barely even lift myself from the couch. I grab my single crutch and hobble over to the door in order to let him in.

"Hey," he says softly.

"Hey," I say back.

"Do you mind if I come in?" he asks.

I open the door wider, indicate the living room with the tip of my crutch.

"Isn't this great?" I say, displaying my crutch as if it

is some kind of great fashion accessory. "As if I didn't look ridiculous enough already, now I can be Pregnant Girl with a Crutch."

"I think you look wonderful," he says. Seated on the couch, he looks nervous.

"Do you want to take off your coat?" I offer.

"Oh. Right," he says. But when he goes to remove the sleeves, he forgets to switch the green cone-shaped thing in his hand to the other side and the sleeve of his coat gets caught on it.

"Oh, *duh*," he says, holding it out for me. "These are for you."

I take the crinkly green paper and look inside. There are roses inside, a pale purple color, and as I lift them to my nose, I vaguely remember once-upon-a-time telling Danny that purple was my favorite color.

"I better put these in water," I say.

"No, let me," he says. He points to the crutch. "It's probably not all that easy for you to get around on that thing and carry stuff at the same time. Just tell me where I can find something to put them in."

It feels strange—*surreal*, my Creative Writing teacher would say—standing in my kitchen, leaning on a crutch, while I direct Danny Stanton on where to find a vase.

"That's perfect," I say when he sets the flowers, now in their crystal vase, down in the middle of the kitchen table. "They're beautiful. Thanks." I feel so awkward. "Can I get you something to eat? Something to drink?"

"Shouldn't you be sitting down?" he says.

"Maybe," I admit, thinking that mostly I should be sitting down because it is such a shock to see him here.

He gently takes my elbow, as though I am something fragile or special, and leads me back to the couch in the living room, where he seats me on the couch before sitting down right next to me.

"Listen," he says, "I'm so sorry about everything that happened."

"That's okay," I say. "It wasn't like it was anybody's fault. Well, except maybe for that woman who ran the red light and slammed into me."

"Yeah, but if Ricky hadn't gotten you so upset," he says, "none of that ever would have happened."

"Yeah, well . . ."

"You know, I tried to see you at the hospital."

"You *did*?" This is totally news to me.

"Of course. I chased after you when you ran out, I saw you get hit, I used my cell phone to call 911, waited with you until the ambulance came, followed you to the hospital. I tried to see you. I came every day you were there, but your parents kept saying no."

For a moment I am incredibly angry with my parents. But then, for whatever reason, the anger fades as quickly as it came.

"Did they say why?" I ask.

"They said they had no way of knowing why you left the dance so quickly after getting there. I think they were worried it was my fault somehow, but they had no way of knowing what really happened."

It is hard to believe that my parents never once mentioned Danny trying to see me, never once asked me straight-out if he had anything to do with it or not. It is hard sometimes to understand why parents ever do the things they do, and I wonder if I will ever understand them.

At last I shrug my shoulders. "Parents," I say.

"Yeah," Danny says, as if he knows exactly what I am talking about.

"So," I say, "why did you keep trying to see me?"

Now Danny looks agitated, as if I am just not *getting* something.

"Because I was sorry!" he says. "Didn't I already say that?"

"And I already said the accident wasn't your fault. It was just one of those stupid things that happen."

"Not just that!" he says. "I'm sorry about everything!"

"I don't understand."

"What part of 'everything' don't you understand?"

"Well," I laugh, "everything."

And he is suddenly laughing too. "Yeah," he says, "that would about cover it." Then he turns serious again. "It's like this: I'm sorry for being such a jerk before. I'm sorry for all those months I didn't talk to you. I'm sorry I didn't see what you were going through. I'm just plain sorry I didn't *see* you."

Even though we saw each other every day at school, even though we are technically seeing each other right now, I know instinctively he is talking about something else.

I try another laugh. "So it took me almost getting myself killed and dying for you to see me?"

176

He shakes his head. At me? At himself? "No, I think I used to see you, but somehow I forgot how. I was too busy seeing my own fucked-up *bullshit* for too long to see anything else. But I see you now, Angel."

Maybe it is the pregnancy hormones I am always reading about, but I feel tears come to my eyes.

"I broke up with Ricky," he says.

"It wasn't really her fault what happened," I say.

"No, I know that," he says. "Still, I broke up with her."

I don't ask why he went out with her so long in the first place, if he thinks he would ever get back together with her again. Somehow I think the answer must be no.

"You're my best friend, Angel," he says.

The tears come to my eyes again. I think I understand what he is saying. A part of me feels like I know him so well, have always known him so well. But I need to hear him explain it to me.

"Why?" I ask.

"Remember what I said to you the night of Ricky's party at the end of the summer?"

"I think I do," I say cautiously. Then I try to turn the sudden seriousness of this into a joke. "You mean when you said how much you like beer?"

"Did I say that?" He shakes his head. "No. I mean, yes, I do like beer. But, no, that's not it. I said that the thing I liked best about you is that you don't care at all, not about stupid stuff like me playing basketball, how if I stopped playing tomorrow, it wouldn't matter to you at all. And I don't think it would matter to you, not unless it mattered to me."

I nod, because it's true.

"Everyone else," he says, "they care about what I can *do*. They don't care about who I *am*."

I nod again.

"Sometimes I think," he says, "that all that stuff we used to do, you and me, just hooking up together occasionally at parties, never getting serious, was because the very idea of you scared me, Angel, I liked you so much. It was easier just to go on being what everyone else saw in me. What I felt for you was too real. *You* were too real."

Then Danny Stanton reaches out a hand, covers one of mine with his.

"You're my best friend, Angel," he says again. "I want to be there for you now."

march

TAKING LAMAZE CLASSES WITH DANNY STANTON AS MY coach may qualify as the weirdest thing I've ever done.

But Danny keeps insisting he wants to be there for me, and when I say I am starting Lamaze classes, he says he wants to come along too.

"They have classes to teach you how to have a baby?" he says. "Who knew?"

When Dr. Caldwell told me about the Lamaze classes, she said it would be better if I had a coach.

"Sure, you can try to do it by yourself," she said, "or you can even hire a doula, someone who makes a profession out of helping women give birth. But most people prefer to have someone they know with them during labor and delivery. And it's much better when you're taking the classes if you have someone else there with you to help with the breathing exercises and to function as a second set of ears when the instructor's talking."

I had thought long and hard over whom I could ask. I thought about asking my mom, but then my dad would feel left out, and besides, things are still not all that great between me and her, not like they used to be. I thought about asking Aunt Stacey—which seemed like almost the perfect choice, because she has been so perfect and so cool about everything with me—but then my mom would be hurt. And of course there was always Karin, who I still think of as my best friend—my best *girl*friend at any rate—but things have been so distant between us for so long, I worried she would say no or, worse, go ahead and do it even though her heart wasn't really in it.

So of course Danny offered to go with me, and then of course *everyone* was offended.

"Wouldn't you rather have me there?" my mother asks. "Why would you want to have *him* there?"

I know that my mom and dad have been thinking Danny must still be feeling guilty about what happened on the night of the Valentine's Day dance, that he must be responsible somehow. After all, they're probably thinking, why else would he be spending time with me now, why would he want to go through any of this with me at all if he didn't feel like he had to?

No matter how many times I tell them this isn't the case, I can tell they still think it is.

"Because," I tell my mom, "he's the first person besides me to show any real enthusiasm about this."

But I am less enthusiastic about this myself when we get to the class that is held in one of the conference rooms at the hospital. I am less enthusiastic because while it is one thing to read descriptions and see pictures of childbirth in a paperback book that measures eight inches by eleven, it is quite another thing to see it projected on a large screen. I am less enthusiastic because it is one thing to think, in theory, that it would be cool to have Danny Stanton in the labor and delivery rooms with me, and quite another to picture him beside me, holding my hand as I scream my bloody head off like the lady on the screen is doing every time she's not panting like a dog.

"You can back out any time," I lean over and whisper to him.

"Are you kidding me?" he says, eyes glued to the

screen as he slouches in his seat, arms crossed. "This is way cool."

The Lamaze instructor flicks on the lights, and she talks to us about some of the things we will need to know, repeating some of the material I have already read in the book. She talks about when to call the hospital, about centimeters and dilation, she talks about back labor, which sounds positively awful.

As she talks, I look around the room at the six other couples there. The women are on a continuum of largeness, but I know it is impossible to tell where people are in their pregnancies until the Lamaze instructor does roll call by due dates; some women gain a lot, some can be due in a week and still look like they've hardly gained at all.

The couples are all older than Danny and I, some by a little, some by a lot. All the women have wedding rings on, except for one whose fingers are swollen up like sausages from all the water retention, but I can see from the white band of skin around her finger that she has one somewhere too; she just can't wear it right now. I know this does not really speak for society at large, that plenty of unmarried people have kids—single people, even gay people—but it still feels odd being the only one, except for the woman who can't wear hers, without a ring in here.

It is nice that Danny wants to be here, but I am so used to feeling as though I am alone in this, it is a little hard to make space for someone else in this picture. And then I ask myself, *Can he really want to be here? Isn't he maybe just trying to be nice?*

I lean over toward him again, whisper again. "Really," I say, "you can back out at any time."

"Are you kidding me?" he says. "I can't believe how *cool* this is."

I study Danny's profile as he listens with as much attention as any of the real fathers there, that face I know so well, love so much.

I tell myself not to get my hopes up, not ever, not about anything.

I tell myself this could be just a passing phase for Danny Stanton, a flight of fancy. For him maybe this is just a new hobby. But, for me, this is my life.

Week of March 11/Week 28

Being finally back at school is no different from how it was before. Or maybe it is different, a little bit. Before,

I was The Girl Who Isn't Smart Enough to Have an Abortion. Now I am The Girl Who Isn't Smart Enough to Have an Abortion and Who Was Also Stupid Enough to Get in a Car Accident. Except for Joshua Carr, who keeps trying to be my friend, and Kelly Bergstrom and John Paul Johnson, who are still hoping I will become a charter member of Students 4 Life, everyone cuts a wide detour around me in the halls.

At least Robin Keating is glad to see me back.

"I've been looking into special programs at the community college for you," he says. "It's still not Yale, but I see where they have some kind of writer-in-residence program sponsored by the National Endowment for the Arts that attracts at least one name author each year. I'm thinking that could at least be good."

"Thanks," I say.

When I see Karin, I don't ask her why she hasn't been to visit me. Maybe she has just been busy with studying, with Todd, I tell myself.

In the cafeteria, I am waiting in line to pay for my salad and turkey sandwich when Ricky D'Amico brushes past me from behind.

If I had thought about this encounter in advance, I

suppose I would have guessed she would be embarrassed by what happened. But she doesn't look embarrassed at all. If anything, she only looks sorry she didn't just knock me over. And she looks angry. I figure she must blame me for her breakup with Danny.

"Could you *be* taking up any more space?" she says to me, walking past with her tray.

And then I hear, from behind me, "Hey. Ricky. Cut it out."

It's Danny's voice. Then he adds, looking right at Ricky, "Could you *be* any ruder?"

She looks at us both in disgust, as if we are one person, before walking off to sit with her friends.

"Here," Danny says, taking my tray out of my hands so that now he is holding both of our trays, one in each hand, "let me get that for you."

He leads me over to a long table where no one else is sitting, sets down our trays. If there were proper seats here and not benches, I swear he would pull out my seat for me.

All around us I feel the air in the room change as Danny starts talking to me.

"So what was Keating saying to you before?" he

asks, biting into his burger, not even noticing that everyone is staring at us.

I tell him about the writing program at the community college.

"That could be cool," he says, "but I know how much you had your heart set on Yale. I mean, me? I'll go, I'll play ball somewhere, hopefully I'll get okay grades. But you? You were lined up for the big time."

"Yeah, well."

In a school where there's a new rumor every day, it doesn't take long for the whispers to start up again, and into the silence following my "Yeah, well" I hear some guy sitting behind Danny say, "What the *hell* is he doing with her?"

And Danny, who has never worried about what anyone else thinks, who has never had to worry about what anyone else thinks, because he is in fact Danny Stanton, spins in his seat.

"Hey, asshole," he says, "what the hell are you staring at?"

And then something happens that I never would have thought would happen in this cafeteria, not in a million years: Danny reaches across the table with his hand, takes my hand in his.

I am holding hands in public with Danny Stanton.

And it is such a deliberate act, his taking my hand like that, that I'm shocked. What will doing this cost him? Will it cost him anything?

I think about the things we do and how every single thing we do in this life matters. Nothing is without consequence. That doesn't mean a person shouldn't act. If we thought and rethought every single thing before doing it, no one would ever act. We'd all be Hamlet, or so my Creative Writing teacher says. But we do need to weigh things *enough*, and this means that there are always at least two paths from any given point and we should always try to choose the better of the two.

I look at Danny's hand holding my hand and, thinking about what it means to live deliberately, I make a choice and squeeze back.

Week of March 18/Week 29

My mother says we should do something to mark my eighteenth birthday.

I tell her this will be great if only I can stop peeing long enough to enjoy it. Now that I am into my third trimester, the bathroom and I have become best buds and I need to stop myself from laughing too hard at anything because it is always possible that urine disaster will ensue.

We have always had family parties to celebrate my birthday, going back as far as I can remember. In the family photo albums there are pictures of me smearing pink frosting on myself when I turned one, me getting my first bike with training wheels at age three, and last year a family party that combined my relatives and friends from school.

Of course, up until last year when we combined the two, I have always celebrated with my friends as well: the duckpin bowling party when I turned five, the manicure party when I turned eight, the sweet-sixteen party, held at home, where my parents even had a band playing in the garage.

This year, of course, I have no interest in or intention of going out partying. It is enough, at this point, to be able to reach my own toenails in order to clip and paint them, to see my shoes when I stand up, to find a comfortable position so the nearly constant back pain eases a bit.

"Eighteen is an important year," my mom says. "You should have whomever you want here."

Then she tells me she's already invited Karin.

Well, why wouldn't she? Karin has always been at my parties, whether for friends or just family.

"I talked to Karin's mother," my mom says, "and she said yes, that Karin would love to come."

A part of me wonders if Karin's mother asked Karin first, wonders if Karin would have said yes so eagerly if it had been left up to her.

"Naturally," my mother adds, "you can invite anyone else you want to. Maybe you'd like to invite some of the other kids from school?"

But, of course, there is only one person from school I want to invite: I surprise myself by getting up the nerve to invite Danny Stanton, and he surprises me by saying yes right away.

Even though I know my parents must have told the rest of the family about my pregnancy, even though they all sent cards when I was in the hospital and recovering afterward, with the exception of Aunt Stacey, this will be the first time I am seeing everybody since Christmas. And even then I didn't really see them, being hidden away most of the time up in my room.

It is strange how they are with me when they arrive. I have known all of them my whole life, and yet now it is as though I am an entirely different person to them. Except for Aunt Stacey no one asks directly about the baby. I could be wearing a beach ball under my blouse or a time bomb they need to avoid.

Karin arrives before anyone else, because my mother has asked her to come early, probably assuming we would want to spend time alone together talking about whatever we have always talked to each other about first, before everyone else arrives.

But Karin doesn't appear to have anything to say to me, and she spends the pre-party time helping my parents put things out on the table: fresh veggies, chips and dip, cheese and crackers.

It is later, with everyone else seated around the table to eat—eggplant parmesan, pasta, all of my current favorites—when the doorbell rings one last time.

"I'll get it," I say, struggling to my feet.

It's Danny, his hair carefully combed, a sloppily wrapped present in his hands.

"Sorry I'm late," he says. "You don't know how

190

many tries it took me to wrap this thing."

When my parents see who is at the door, they are both obviously upset.

"You didn't say . . . Danny was coming," my mom says.

"You should have said something," my dad says.

Even though his being there bothers them, they would never say any more in front of the relatives, in front of Karin, than this. I know they are upset to see him there because they still blame him for a lot of things. Plus, my mom is still resentful that Danny is the one going with me to Lamaze classes.

Karin is visibly thrown by Danny being there too. Even though she must have seen us talking together in school the past few weeks, even though she was in the cafeteria the day he told off Ricky and sat down with me, I'm sure she never expected to see him here, not at my eighteenth birthday party. The way things used to be, Danny Stanton would never have been here with me like this with my family. *It is funny,* I think sometimes, *how invested people become in seeing you as you were, and how hard it is for them to see you as you are.*

My grandmother, who has always seemed to me

to be a bit oblivious anyway, fails to see the sudden tension in the room.

"Sit, sit," Grandmother Hansen says to Danny, pulling up a seat for him beside her and placing food on his plate even before he can sit down.

Later, when we are clearing the table, Grandmother Hansen stops me in the kitchen.

"Such a nice boy," she says, "that Danny. You and I should talk sometime. Soon."

Still later, we are opening presents on the living room floor before having cake.

My aunts and uncles, grandparents and cousins, all give me the kind of practical things they've been giving me for years: cash, savings bonds, gift certificates for clothing and music stores. No one ever thinks to give me gift certificates to bookstores, which I would really love.

My mom and dad give me a basket filled with school supplies: pens and paper, of course, but also a computer program for screenplay writing.

"It's for later," my dad says. "You know, afterward," meaning the baby.

"I know you say you want to write novels," my mom

says, my literary-aspirations cat having popped out of its bag, "but it can't hurt to stretch yourself in different directions."

"I guess not," I say, and laugh, patting my belly. "I'm obviously stretching in all kinds of directions."

They look horrified at this.

"Seriously," I say, "thanks."

Then Karin gives me her present. It's a top from our favorite store at the mall. It is purple with a halter on top, but just below the breasts the material is filmy, so it has the effect of looking like something a genie on the beach might wear. It is exactly the kind of thing I would pick out for myself, except . . .

I hold it up to my body. There are a couple of inches of me spreading out on either side of the narrow cut.

"I didn't think—," Karin starts.

"That's okay," I say, and smile. "I'll save it for some-time afterward. Really, it's perfect."

My mom says it's time for cake and we are all getting up when Grandmother Hansen says, "What's this? You forgot to open one of your presents."

In her hands is the sloppily wrapped present Danny arrived with, that he'd put off to one side, and

I open it as everyone sits back down again.

There are three things inside. The first is a journal with a leather cover and gold-tipped pages.

"I guess this is really the same kind of thing your folks got you," Danny says. "I guess I just thought it might be nice for you to have somewhere you could write whatever you want, maybe even write about the baby."

I see my relatives thinking, see Karin thinking, *How does he know about Angel's writing?*

The second thing is a baby blanket that feels soft against my cheek and is as purely white as the snow was the day Danny came to visit me after the accident.

Now Danny is starting to look embarrassed. For someone who is used to having all that attention focused on him on the basketball court, he has trouble dealing with all this attention in my living room now.

"I know you said you didn't want any kind of shower," Danny says. And again I see my relatives thinking, see Karin thinking, *How does he know these things?* "But I thought you should have something special for the baby."

The third thing is a purple ribbon to tie back my hair. If Danny was on his way to embarrassed before, he is totally there now, but that doesn't stop him from speaking. "I was reading this Web site online," he says, coughing into his hand to clear his throat, "and it said that women, when they get into the later part of their pregnancies, like to feel as though they're still pretty, still themselves, like they're more than just a person carrying a baby."

My family has no idea what to do with Danny, what to do with any of this, so we do what we always do when we don't know what else to do. We eat; in this instance, cake.

"Make a wish?" my mother says as the candle burns.

But right now there is nothing else I want other than what I have already, in this moment. Or maybe there is one thing I want, but I tell myself that Danny Stanton is only being so nice to me because, maybe, Danny Stanton is just an incredibly nice person after all.

I blow out the candle, wishless, and think this is certainly the strangest birthday party I have ever had.

Week of March 25/Week 30

I tell myself this is not a date, that Danny is just being friendly when he asks me if I want to see a movie with him on Friday night, especially when he adds that Karin and Todd will be going too.

Karin acts strangely from the minute I get into the car with them. I think maybe it is because she got used to having Ricky there whenever she went out with Danny and Todd.

I have never asked Karin what that was like, being with Danny and Ricky. I didn't want to know, still don't.

I am so excited to be doing this, doing something that feels *normal*, that I do not even care what movie we are going to see and am surprised when it turns out to be a romantic comedy, which would normally be a good thing but which in my present pee-happy condition presents a dilemma.

The heroine in the movie is something of a ditz, and she keeps finding herself thrown together in situations with this guy she keeps telling everyone she dislikes. She trips over a curb and falls at his feet, she accidentally sets fire to her apartment and he has to save her, and the whole time it is hard to believe she is unaware of the most obvious fact: She is in love with him.

But none of that matters as I sit in the darkened

movie theater eating my popcorn. In all the time I have known Danny we have never done something so simple as go to the movies together, not since that first date years ago.

Afterward Danny suggests we go to the diner. I say yes even though now that I am into my third trimester, what Dr. Caldwell predicted, has happened. The baby is taking up so much space inside me now, I find I can only eat small meals at a time, otherwise I get heartburn, and the popcorn has totally filled me up.

But I am just happy to be here, even if Karin barely talks to me, even if Ricky D'Amico glares at us as she walks by our table.

Danny is oblivious to Karin's silence, oblivious to Ricky's glare. He is content just to eat his cheeseburger, and I am content to watch him eat it.

Danny asks if we want to go anywhere else. Maybe we could take a drive to the lake?

But Karin says no.

"Thanks," she says, "but I'm kind of beat. Maybe you could just drop Todd and me at my house?"

"How about you?" Danny asks after we drop them. "Do you want to go to the lake?"

The idea of being alone with Danny at the lake sounds heavenly, but now that I am in my third trimester I get tired easily, and it is well past my new bedtime.

"Another time?" I say as I yawn, barely able to keep my eyes open.

When we get to my house, Danny walks me to the door, the porch light guiding our path.

"This was great," he says.

"It was," I say, and smile sleepily.

"We should do this again sometime," he says.

I am brought up short by that "sometime." It is such a vague word.

Then Danny leans down to my short height from his far greater one, and his face is just a breath away from me.

"I've never kissed a pregnant girl before," Danny says, right before he does exactly that, his lips gently touching mine.

When he pulls away, I think of how what he just said must be true: Of all the girls Danny Stanton has kissed, and there have been a lot, I must surely be the first one who is seven months pregnant.

Then he touches his lips to mine again and the kiss

turns into something else, something more like the way he used to kiss me when we used to hook up at parties occasionally, only different. This kiss is deeper somehow. It feels, in a way, as though he is trying to read me, as though I am trying to read him.

I don't want the moment to end, not ever, but I feel Danny pull away.

"Well," he says, "I guess I better get going. You need your sleep."

"Okay," I say.

As I watch him walk away, I tell myself that this must just be some kind of novelty to him, that whatever that kiss just meant to me, it couldn't possibly mean the same thing to him.

april

THE VERY IDEA OF BREAST-FEEDING FEELS LIKE AN APRIL
Fool's joke.

What kind of God would invent such a thing? I think, as I listen to the midwife from Dr. Caldwell's practice give her mini-lecture. *If we need to ensure the survival of the species, since women already have to give birth to the babies, shouldn't guys somehow be able to do this part? Okay, so maybe guys would look really stupid with breasts, but couldn't babies just feed out of, oh, I don't know, guys' fingers or something?*

I have taken the day off from school to be here. The breast-feeding clinic is only held on weekdays, and Dr. Caldwell thinks it's a good idea for me to go.

"You can learn a lot from books," she tells me, "but sometimes books aren't half as good as talking to real people."

So I sit with the other women as June Kaye, the

midwife from Dr. Caldwell's practice, regales us with the superiority of breast over bottle.

I remember when Karin and I first started getting breasts, not long before my first period when I was eleven. I remember how confused and excited we both were. It was like our bodies, in changing like this, were doing things beyond our control. Plus, it was weird having breasts so young. It was kind of embarrassing at school, as though we'd somehow done something wrong to make our bodies turn out like this, so soon. But it also felt totally cool, and powerful in a weird way, like we were doing something unique, even if every other woman in the history of the world had already done the same thing before us. We were the first people to ever have breasts. Certainly, we were the first people to ever buy bras.

"That white one with the pink bow in the middle sure is nice, Mrs. Hansen," Karin said, "but don't you think this light purple one is more . . . *Angel*?"

My mother wound up buying two each for Karin and me—we each got one of the ones my mom thought we should have, and we each got one of the ones Karin thought would be better—before we headed off to the food court for pizza and diet sodas. Back then my mom always treated Karin like a second daughter, and Karin could always talk my mom into just about anything.

"Breast is best," I begin to think now, listening to June Kaye talk, is a catchphrase I could soon grow to hate.

I look around at the other women at the breast-feeding clinic and wonder what their stories are. They are probably all married, or most are, probably have their nurseries all set up, have families where every single member of those families are excited about what they are going through.

I listen as June Kaye talks about something called "proper latch," as she explains pumping, as she talks about the benefits of breast over bottle.

But I can't help it: The idea of a baby attaching itself to my breast like that just totally skeeves me out. It is one thing to do that sort of thing with a guy; it is quite another to have a baby attach itself to you like some kind of tiny alien with strange eating habits.

But as I listen to June Kaye talk, as I hear her talk about the antibodies breast milk gives a baby, about how breast-fed babies have on average eight more IQ points than bottle-fed babies, I think that I want my baby to be as healthy as I can help her be, I want her to have those extra IQ points.

So I will try this thing. If it doesn't work out—and June Kaye does say that sometimes, for whatever reason, it doesn't work out—I won't beat myself up about it.

It's simply that, now that I know about those antibodies and those extra IQ points, I can't choose otherwise.

Week of April 8/Week 32

Back on my birthday my grandmother said she wanted to have a little talk with me sometime. And now Grandmother Hansen, a woman who despite sometimes seeming a little bit out of it has been known to beat the tables at both Atlantic City *and* Vegas, calls in her marker.

"When you were little," she says, "you used to come here all the time. So now that you're so big"—in more ways than one, I think—"you can't come visit your grandmother anymore?"

She's right, of course. When I was little I was over her place all the time. Even though my mother works from home, having me underfoot wasn't always the easiest thing when she had lots of client appointments at the house, so up until around the time I turned nine, my grandmother would pick me up after ballet class, taking me back to her house to do my homework and have a snack.

"I know you girls all want to be skinny these days," she'd say. "But have a cookie."

"If I have too many cookies," I'd say, "I won't look very good in my costumes."

"Are you planning on being a professional ballerina?" she'd say.

"No," I'd say, and shake my head.

"So?" she'd say. "Then have the cookie *and* dance. What's the matter? You never learned to keep two opposing views in your mind at the same time?"

She was right about the cookies and dancing, and she's right now. I owe her a visit.

"Do you have any cookies?" I ask her over the phone.

"Chocolate chip or oatmeal raisin?" she asks.

I really want the former, but . . .

"Oatmeal raisin," I say, thinking of the baby.

"Well, I have both," she says, "so you don't need to make up your mind right now."

Her kitchen, when I get there, is so familiar: the pale yellow walls, the wooden table and chairs, the cookie jar in the middle of the table, the scent of fresh-baked cookies in the air.

"Sit," she says. "Milk, right?" she says, waving the carton in the air.

I nod.

She sets out plates, takes the lid off the cookie jar.

"Chocolate chip or oatmeal raisin?" she asks again.

"Oatmeal raisin," I say.

"But you like chocolate chip better."

"But oatmeal raisin's probably better for the baby. You know—oatmeal? Raisins? As opposed to chips, chocolate?"

She laughs, puts one of each on my plate.

"You're just like your mother was when she had you," she says. "So many things people worry about these days. One chocolate chip cookie won't hurt the baby."

As I bite into the cookie, the taste of butter and chocolate warm in my mouth, I think maybe she's right.

"Your mother used to worry about everything when she was pregnant with you," Grandmother Hansen says, breaking her own cookie in half.

"What were they like back then?" I ask.

"Your parents?"

I nod.

"Well, they were young, of course, older than you are now, but still young. And so sure of themselves! You couldn't tell them anything. Or at least I couldn't. 'Helena's read all the baby books,' your father would say. 'People do things differently these days from how you and Dad did them.'"

I wince for her sake. *Ouch.*

"Exactly." She laughs. "I mean, it *was* annoying. I'd raised three kids myself—your grandfather was hardly ever home back then, he worked so hard—and they didn't think I knew anything."

"You must have been pissed," I say, not thinking.

"Pissed?" She laughs again. "Oh, maybe. But I could see how determined your parents were, how sure they were that they were making all the right decisions. And they both wanted you, so very much."

It's funny. I suppose my whole life I have taken for

206

granted my parents' having me, but I have never really thought before of them *wanting* me, much less "very much."

"And your parents were right in a certain sense," Grandmother Hansen says. "Things *were* different for them."

"How so?"

"They decided they wanted to have a baby, so they got pregnant and had a baby."

"How was that different?"

Grandmother Hansen looks as though she is debating something with herself, deciding whether to say the next thing or not.

"This is something I never told anyone else," she says. "Your grandfather doesn't know. And, of course, I never told your father."

I don't say anything, worried that if I speak she'll change her mind.

"I didn't really want your father," she says.

This comes as a total shock. There has never been anything but good feelings between my father and his mother. Oh, sure, they argue and get on each other's nerves sometimes, but don't all parents and kids do that?

"Then why did you have him?" I ask.

"Are you kidding?" she says. "I didn't have a choice. We didn't have options back then, not really. This was before *Roe v. Wade*. And I certainly wasn't going to go to one of those back-alley doctors. My own mother used to tell the story about how, one day, she came home early from school to find *her* mother in the kitchen with some man who had a coat hanger."

This is an awful lot to digest.

"My dad doesn't know any of this?" I say.

"No," she says, "and don't you tell him either."

"I promise."

"It's funny," she says, "but even though I didn't want your dad when I first found out I was pregnant, it's impossible for me now to imagine my life without him in it."

This is her story, not mine, and yet a part of me feels like I understand something of what she is talking about.

"So, tell me, Angel," she says, "because I've never gotten a straight answer from your parents on this, why are you having this baby?"

"In the beginning," I say, "I didn't want the baby at

all, but I just couldn't go through with what it would take to *not* have the baby. I couldn't stop thinking about how all I'd ever done was *react* to things that were happening to me and that having an abortion was just one more reaction. I didn't want to live like that anymore. I didn't want to have any more regrets, so I made a choice. At first, though, I assumed I'd probably just put it up for adoption, but something changed along the way. Somewhere the baby stopped being an *it* to me, an *idea*, and now I do want to keep my baby, very much so."

"That," she says, "is probably as good a reason as any."

Week of April 15/Week 33

Since Danny gave me this journal, I have been scared in a way to open it. I love looking at the leather and gold-tipped pages, love thinking of him picking this out for me. But I suppose I have been scared to put pen to paper, thinking whatever I might write wouldn't be worthy of the gift. At last I finally do so, because I have something I want to write about Danny.

The prom is coming up in five weeks. I guess that seems a silly first sentence to have in this book, but it's true. I don't know what I was thinking about the prom. Certainly, I didn't think I'd be going. I guess I just figured that I would stay home that night, maybe watch a little TV with my parents, that hopefully Karin would tell me all about it later: what people wore, who won King and Queen, who vomited on their gowns and tuxes.

Karin is, of course, going with Todd for sure. I kept wondering who Danny was going to ask—surely he would go with someone; it was his senior prom, after all—but Danny and I have not talked much since the night he kissed me after the movies, except to talk about pregnancy stuff, so it'd feel funny asking him who he was taking. And, anyway, it would be too awful to listen as he named some other girl's name. I know I could have asked Karin—through Todd, she'd know; they are probably all going together—but I don't want to do that, either. It would be only barely less awful hearing it from Karin than hearing it from Danny.

Then, yesterday, in the cafeteria, I got my answer.

I was sitting at a table by myself next to one where Danny was sitting with all his basketball buddies.

Danny actually did ask me if I wanted to sit with them when he saw me walking by, but I just shook my head, no. I may be okay with spending time alone with Danny, but it would feel too weird being with his friends too, being the way I am now.

Then, as I was watching Danny laughing at something someone said, I saw Ricky D'Amico slink in from behind him, putting one leg over the bench and squeezing in between him and the guy he was sitting closest to.

Danny looked surprised to see her right there, so close, but he didn't try to move away.

"Hey, Stanton," I heard Ricky say, clear as anything. "You. Me. The prom. I'll pay for the limo."

Give her credit: She had more nerve than I would ever have. I would never be brave enough to go so nakedly after something I wanted.

Danny looked shocked, and then I saw him smile and open his mouth to speak.

I quickly picked up my tray and awkwardly climbed off the bench, moving as fast as my body would let me toward the trash, because of all the things I'd ever wanted to hear come out of Danny Stanton's mouth, I did not want to hear him say yes to Ricky D'Amico.

I was trying to get everything off my tray into the trash — Why was that damn fry stuck to the orange plastic? Why wouldn't it just come off? — when Joshua Carr came up behind me.

"I've been looking for you," he said.

"You have," I said, half-surprised, but more concerned with getting that last fry off my tray, with getting away from Danny and Ricky as quickly as was humanly possible. "Well, you found me," I said.

"I want to take you to the prom," Joshua blurted out.

"What?"

"I want you to go with me," he said, gaining more confidence, even though he did sort of look like someone would look if they were about to eat broccoli when they hated broccoli.

And in that look I could see what was going on. Joshua Carr still felt sorry for me. He felt it was the do-gooder thing to do, making it so I could go just like anybody else.

And I was tempted. If Joshua wanted to take me to the prom with him, fine, I thought, I'd go. So what if

212

his reasons weren't exactly flattering. At least I'd get to go to my senior prom, see what all the fuss was about for myself.

But even as I was getting ready to answer yes, I could feel my eyes being drawn to Danny and Ricky.

"No," I told Joshua.

"No?"

"Look, I'm sorry," I said. "I know you meant well, but no, although I do thank you for asking."

Even though Joshua was surprised by my answer— how could I have turned him down?—he also looked relieved as he walked away, like one of those fish I used to let go whenever I went fishing with my dad when I was a little girl.

I looked at Danny and Ricky, still sitting there together, thinking how they would be going to the prom together, how I would be staying home alone. And it was okay. Okay, so maybe it wasn't totally okay— maybe it was awful—but I realized then that I would rather stay home alone than go with Joshua Carr, since being with Joshua Carr was not where I wanted to be, since the only place I really wanted to be was with Danny.

And as I sit here now and write this, I think about how everything we do somehow comes down to the choices we make. It is like life is a series of street corners, one immediately after the other, and at each of those corners there are only ever really two choices — a better choice and a worse choice — and I think how whatever we choose at any given point in time somehow influences every single thing that comes afterward.

As I write about making choices, I remember what my grandmother said, what Aunt Stacey said, and I begin to see a pattern here. I see that we are all part of a continuum of experience, yet each of us experiences things wholly for ourselves.

And I begin to see something else.

I think that I have been so busy worrying about what others see when they look at me, worrying that I am not really seen at all, that I have failed to notice the obvious. Whatever Karin appears to be on the surface, she is not what she seems either. She is not simply angry with me, or bored with me, or just too busy with Todd. There is something else going on here.

I pound on Karin's door so hard and fast, it is as though I might break it down.

When Karin throws open the door, Todd is standing right there behind her.

"Angel?" she says. "What's wrong? Is something wrong with the baby?"

"No." I shake my head, puzzled. "If something was wrong with the baby, why wouldn't I just go straight to the hospital?"

She looks relieved at first, then the anger and dismissal I've become accustomed to settles into her features.

"What is it, then?" she says. "What were you pounding so loud for?"

I turn to Todd. "Would you excuse us, please?" I ask nicely.

"Hey!" Karin says. "You can't just tell him to go!"

"I didn't tell him to go," I point out. "I asked him to excuse us, meaning he could just go to some other room. Of course, if he wants to go walk around for a bit, that's fine too."

"Where do you get off?" Karin says.

"Look," I say, "he's had all your attention for the last several months, and as far as I'm concerned, he can have it back again later for as long as you two want, forever even. I just want a few minutes of your time. Alone. That's all."

Before Karin can protest any more, Todd kisses her on the top of her head. "That's cool," he says. "Later," he says, brushing past me.

"What?" she says when he's gone, sounding both angry and tired now. "What is it?"

"What happened," I say, "to us?"

"I don't know what you're talking about," she says, as though I might be nuts. "What are you talking about?"

"We used to be so . . . close," I say.

"So?" she says. "So maybe we grew apart a bit. So? These things happen all the time."

"Not to us," I say. "This was never supposed to happen to us."

"People change," she says.

"Maybe," I say, "but the friendship doesn't."

"I think you're making a big deal out of nothing," she says.

"I don't think so," I say. "We were never nothing. Tell

216

me this, because I really want to know: What changed between us after I decided to keep the baby?"

"You didn't just decide to *keep* the baby!" She bursts out with it, and there is a half cry in her words. "You decided *not* to get an abortion!"

"I still don't understand," I say, and I don't, not yet. "Why should that change things between *us*?"

"Because what you did was *different* from what I did! And every time I look at you now, it's like an *indictment* of me, a *judgment* against me! It's too hard to look at you, Angel. I just feel like you're . . . *judging* me all the time!"

I finally do see what she's saying now, and even though I see how much it costs her to say it, I still don't like the words.

"You don't really get it at all, do you?" I say. "I don't *care* what you did. I mean, of course I care, in the same way that I care about everything that happens to you, but I'm not sitting here judging you all the time. What kind of person do you think I am?"

She doesn't say anything.

"You did what you did, and I did what I did. So we chose differently. We're different people. Where's the surprise there? We each did the best we could. We each did what we needed to do."

Still she says nothing.

"Why does it always have to be like this?" I say. "Why does what one person does have to seem like some kind of judgment against other people? I don't *want* to choose for everybody else," I finally say. "It's too much responsibility. Just for me. I just want the right to choose for me."

And then I can't take it anymore.

I go to Karin. I put my arms around the best girlfriend I have ever known in my whole life, and I hold her close. I will keep standing here for as long as it takes, until she remembers what this is like, until she hugs me back.

Week of April 29/Week 35

Now that it's so close to the end, I am tired most of the time, and it doesn't help that, unable to get comfortable anymore when I lie down, I'm having difficulty sleeping at night.

Into my weekend-morning sleepiness, my dad says he wants to go fishing with me.

"Are you sure that's such a good idea?" my mom says. "Do you really think it's wise for her to be out in your leaky boat in her condition?"

"It's not a leaky boat," he says. "And besides, who knows when we'll get another chance?"

Ever since I was small enough to be taken somewhere without needing a diaper bag, my dad has taken me fishing with him.

"Your mother hates fishing," he would say. "And I see enough of other lawyers during the week and on the golf course. I don't need to spend time in a small boat with them on the weekends as well."

Family legend has it that the very first time my dad took me, all I had for a pole was an old bamboo stick with a string attached, and I wouldn't even let my dad put a worm on the hook for me, never mind my putting the worm there myself.

I hated the way those worms looked, dangling there, harpooned by the point of the sharp hook. Somehow I didn't mind the worms on my dad's expensive pole; but I minded the worms on the end of my own bamboo stick very much indeed.

"At least put some bread on the end of the pole," my

dad would say, "give the fish *something* to go for."

But I shook my head and spent that first day fishing just tossing the hook and line over my shoulder before casting it out to sea. I got so bored after a while with the whole exercise — or maybe my childish self thought that somehow what I was doing *was* fishing, that it was all somehow in that back and forth motion — that my dad would say my body just became a thing of continuous motion that day, with no breaks as I tossed that hook and line over my shoulder and flung it back out to sea, back and forth, repeatedly.

At one point, half-mesmerized by the motion, I was shocked to hear my dad yell, "Angel! Stop!" as I was about to cast my line again. "You've got a fish on the end of that thing!"

It was true.

Unlike the salamanders my dad had been fishing up all day long, I'd managed to pull an entire fish out of the sea.

"It's kind of tiny," I remember saying.

"Tiny?" my dad said. "That thing is four inches long!"

My dad always loved that story, would tell it to anyone who would listen, even if they'd heard it before.

"Okay," my mother said, after what must have been the tenth or twelfth time of him telling it. "She caught a fish."

"But she did it without a hook!" my dad would say, holding his index fingers several inches apart, so far you could fit more than that puny fish between them. "It was four inches long!"

"Next year," my dad says now, "we probably won't be able to do this, what with the baby being here by then and all."

And so my dad and I go fishing, for what may be the last time. But unlike the fishing trips of previous years, when my father would take me to places where he said all the best fish hung out—"You're taking her *across state lines*," my mother would say, "for a *fish*?"— my dad is worrying about straying too far with me in my current condition, and so we go to a local place instead.

"Hardly even worth hauling the boat out," he mutters when we get there, as he unropes the boat from the roof of the car, sets it in the water.

"Oh, I don't know." I smile as he delicately hands me in. "You might catch a salamander or two out here."

He rows us out a little ways, careful not to take me too far from shore.

"Worm for that hook?" my dad offers.

"That's okay," I say, taking up my pole. The pole I have now is much nicer than the bamboo pole I used to bring with me. This one has all the bells and whistles on it that any fisherperson could want. "I think I'll just fish naked today."

"You'll probably catch a bigger one than I do," he says, attaching a fancy lure to his own pole.

"Maybe," I say, and shrug.

And then the shrug turns into something else.

"Ow!" I cry out, dropping my pole into the water as my body feels the full violent punch of that something else.

"Angel?" my dad says, dropping to his knees in front of me. "What is it? What's wrong?"

"It was the baby," I say, hand to my stomach, smiling through the pain at the sheer awe of it. "She *kicked* me . . . *hard*!"

"Are you okay?" he asks. I take my father's hand, place it tentatively on my swollen belly.

"There," I say. "Did you feel that? She just did it again!"

At first he looks as though he's unsure he wants to be doing this. Then: "Whoa!" he says. "She's got some kick!"

"You're telling me." As the sensations caused from the kick subside, I realize something. "Shit!" I say. "The pole!"

And there it is in the water, my expensive pole with no worm on it, drifting farther and farther away from the boat.

But my dad doesn't move.

"Aren't you going to go after it?" I say.

"No," he says, and shakes his head. "Angel?"

"What?"

"Have I told you lately how proud I am of you?"

I shake my head.

"I am more damned *proud* to be your father," he says, "than I am of anything else I've ever done in my whole life."

There is nothing adequate I can say in response to this, so I resort back to, "But what about the pole?"

"Oh, to hell with the pole," my dad says, and smiles. "You only would have caught something bigger than me anyway."

may

AT LAMAZE CLASS THERE IS ONE LESS COUPLE THAN WAS there the week before.

"The Carsons had a baby boy," the instructor says. "Mother and John Junior are both doing just fine."

After so many weeks of the group being together, it is strange to think of one of us already having gone through what is still to come for the rest of us, what I think of as going over to the other side.

The instructor takes us on a tour of the facilities. We see the maternity ward, the nursery, the labor and delivery rooms.

"When you come into the hospital," she says, "ask if you can have room number one or room number two. These are our special labor rooms, but no one will offer them to you if you don't ask, so ask. Of course, someone may already be using them—sometimes

224

there's a full house here—but it never hurts to ask."

Then, so we will know what she's talking about, she shows us room number one. It is different from the regular labor rooms. It is much bigger, it is more prettily decorated with light floral wallpaper, and there is an oversize Jacuzzi in the corner.

"That Jacuzzi," the instructor says, "is a wonderful thing."

Danny leans in from the side to whisper in my ear. "I'll bet," he says with a grin. "I could have used one of those after a few of the games we had last season."

Ever since the day I saw Ricky sit down next to Danny in the cafeteria, I have tried to tell him, repeatedly, that he doesn't have to go through any of this with me.

"What are you talking about?" he asked, puzzled. "I *want* to do this with you."

But I thought then, still think, he is doing this out of pity.

"Why the change?" he asked.

But I couldn't tell him, and so he is still with me for this tour.

"That Jacuzzi"—the instructor speaks over Danny's whisper now—"could save you during labor. I don't mean save your life, but it could save you a lot of pain. It's amazing how soothing our laboring mothers find it to sit in that tub between contractions."

I think about the scene she is painting, envision my very pregnant and naked self sitting in that tub with Danny beside me. Rather than seeing me as a bathing beauty, he would see me as a bathing Buddha, and whatever else I might allow Danny to see, I would never let him see me like that.

As the instructor shows us the delivery table with the stirrups on the end of it, points out the uses of the various monitors in the room — machines to make sure the mother is okay, machines to make sure the baby is okay — I think about the missing Carsons and what still lies ahead, how close this all is now. Even though at moments it is still impossible to believe that an entire baby will come out from between my legs, often I feel as if I am on a train that has been stalled on top of the railroad tracks. But soon, very soon, the conductor will release the brake, the train will start speeding down the tracks, and there will be nothing to stop it.

"You look white," Danny says. "Is everything okay?"

I tell him it'll be fine, that I just need some air.

"Come on," he says, taking my hand and leading me out of the hospital. "After all these weeks of classes, if we don't know how to have this baby by now, we never will."

Outside, the night is cool for early May, and something about that coolness makes me feel better, somehow clean again. Even though the evening is relatively early, the stars are strong and I see Orion twinkling overhead, the constellation I painted for the fifth-grade science fair.

"It's funny," I say, neck craned upward, "how that guy never changes."

"Angel?" Danny recalls me to Earth.

I look at him and see that he looks nervous. Danny Stanton, nervous?

"What is it?" I say.

"I've been meaning to ask you," he says. "I've wanted to ask you for weeks: Will you go to the prom with me?"

"*What?*"

"Okay, forget I said anything. I knew maybe it wasn't such a good idea. You're probably going with someone else already. I probably should have asked you sooner."

"But you're going with Ricky D'Amico."

"*What?*"

"I was there, that day in the cafeteria, when she asked you."

"And did you hear me say yes?"

"No," I say, "I left before you said that."

"But I didn't say yes."

"You must have. I saw you. I saw you smile at her after she asked you."

"But you didn't hear me say yes, because I said no."

"But that smile—"

"Was because I was so shocked. I *laughed* at her. It's really too bad you didn't stick around. If you had, then you would have been there to hear it when I said to her, after smiling of course, 'What are you, *nuts*?'"

I think, in that moment, even if it makes me a small person, I would have liked to see the look on Ricky's face when Danny said that. But then I think, *No, he didn't really say that to her . . . did he?*

"No," I say, "you didn't really say that to her . . . did you?"

"Yes!" he says. "I mean, yes, I said no to her. And, yes, I told her she was nuts."

"That probably wasn't your most gallant moment," I say.

"Yeah, well."

I screw up my courage. "And now you're asking me," I say.

"I know I should have asked sooner," Danny says, "but Todd told me he heard someone else say Joshua Carr asked you, and it was a while before I learned from Karin that you said no to him."

Bless Karin.

Danny cranes his own neck up at the night sky, hands deep in his pockets as he studies Orion.

"In a way," he says, "it really is cool the way that, no matter what else changes, he's always just right there like that."

"Danny?" I reach out and place my hand on his shoulder.

He looks down at me.

"Yes?" he says.

"Ask me again."

He takes a deep breath. "Angel, would you go to the prom with me?"

"Yes," I say.

"Yes?"

"Yes."

"Are you there, God? It's me, Angel."

When I was younger, I read that Judy Blume book that all the girls read, *Are You There God? It's Me, Margaret*, the book about the girl who is trying to find her religious place in the world while worrying about when she'll get her first period.

I am thinking of that book, of being that young again, as I open the journal Danny gave me and start to write.

> *I know that some people, certainly Kelly Bergstrom and John Paul Johnson of the Students 4 Life club, think I am doing this because of something having to do with religion.*
>
> *But I don't think that's necessarily so, or at least not in the way they think it is.*
>
> *My family has never been very religious. Oh, sure, we go to church sometimes on the holidays, but it has never been something we discuss very much at home. I do remember thinking, though, when I was very young, that whatever religion our household was must be the <u>right</u> religion, because it was what we thought, and that people who thought differently must have it wrong*

somehow. Then, one holiday when our whole family was here, I realized that even within our small group of people we don't agree on it. I don't recall the exact specifics, but as I listened to Aunt Stacey and Dad debate about heaven, the thought suddenly flashed into my head: Every single person in this room, every single person on the face of the planet, thinks they have the answer and that theirs is the most correct answer. Well, I remember thinking, they can't all be right.

So here is what I think now: I think that God isn't something that exists in some place called heaven. God is something that lives in each human being. God is the choices that live inside us. At any given moment we can move toward the better place in us, or further away from it. And every time we choose for the better, we move closer to God.

That's my belief, anyway.

My mother is surprised when I tell her I am going to the prom.

"Why would you want to put yourself through that?" she asks, and I know she is thinking of what people will say if I go. Maybe she is worrying that I'll be hurt. But then I realize that she must be thinking that I'm planning on going alone, like I did to the Valentine's Day dance, and that I will be hurt again, maybe even worse than before.

"Danny asked me to go with him," I tell her.

"He *did*?"

"But I can go shopping for a dress myself," I say. "Really. It's okay."

I see her make a decision.

"No," she says, with force. "No daughter of mine is going shopping for her prom dress all by herself. This is one of the moments of your life I've been waiting for. We're going to find you the best prom dress ever, and then I'm going to make an appointment with my hairdresser for you to have your hair done that day. I don't want you going to one of those quick-cuts places you're always going to."

But after her high-energy good intentions, once we get to the mall, my mother is a little deflated, because of course we can't get my dress from one of the places displaying gowns in their windows in tiny sizes, where everyone else will get theirs.

We have to get my gown at the maternity store.

"Somehow," she says ruefully, rifling through the oversize evening wear in Mommy Heaven, "this wasn't how I expected this to be."

"Yeah, well," I say, sounding even to my own ears like the oldest person in the world, "almost nothing ever is."

I see my mom's head snap up as she looks at me over the top of the rack. I think she is going to yell at me for my bad attitude, when suddenly she starts to laugh.

"What?" I say.

"Oh, I don't know," she says, sobering. "You know, there have been things about this I didn't understand in the beginning. Sometimes I still don't understand quite how we got here. All I know is, I love you."

"Thanks, Mom," I say. "I think I did know that. But it's always nice to hear."

Week of May 20/Week 38

The doorbell rings and a moment later I hear my dad say, "Danny. You look great. Just a second. I'll go get her."

I hear my dad's tread on the stairs, and he walks into my room just as my mother is brushing a stray hair out of my face. They both stand behind me as I look at my reflection in the full-length mirror hanging on the back of my closet door.

I'm not sure what they see, but I see a girl in a red halter-back ankle-length dress with low heels so she won't trip over them tonight. I see a girl with pretty makeup, with red lipstick and her hair pulled back, tiny gold stars and glitter decorating her dark hair. I see a girl who is enormously pregnant and realize that, whatever else I will be tonight, I will be the only girl at my senior prom who is fully nine months pregnant.

And that is okay.

"Doesn't she look beautiful?" my mom says.

"You stole my words," my dad says.

I make my way carefully down the stairs as Danny waits at the bottom. Standing there in his black tux, white flowers for me in his hands, he is the handsomest thing I have ever seen.

It is a magical moment, the first of what will hopefully be many magical moments this evening.

"You look beautiful," he says. And if I thought my parents were only saying nice parent-speak a moment before, I fully believe him now.

I feel beautiful.

After my parents take what seems like a million pictures, Danny escorts me out to the limo he's ordered for the evening. Even though he said he wasn't planning on drinking tonight, and I certainly can't, he said he didn't want to have to worry about driving, that he wanted to sit back and enjoy the ride.

Danny told me Todd said he and Karin expected to go with us tonight, but that Danny said no. We'd all do something together another time, but tonight he wanted things to be just like this.

When we get to the place where the prom is being held, the Sapphire Room, we stand in line with everyone else to get our official prom pictures taken. Everyone says hi to Danny, some say hi to me, a few even saying "nice dress." When it's our turn, Danny stands behind me, his arms circling me, covering my hands, which are still holding the flowers over my big belly.

Even though we have had other formal parties before, it is always strange seeing everyone dressed up like this, as though they are practicing for who they might become later. And even though we didn't drive here with Karin and Todd, of course we still sit with them during dinner. I know I ordered the chicken instead of the beef for my meal, and when I look down at one point, I see that my plate is empty, but I certainly don't remember doing anything as mundane as eating. I am having too good a time.

Before and after dinner there is dancing. But so far when Danny has asked me, I've said no. As good as I feel, it just seems like it would be too awkward, trying to dance while being so big. Plus, everyone would stare.

It comes time for the crowning of the king and queen, the results to be based on the ballots we all filled out as we came in earlier. When I filled mine out, I couldn't help but notice that Danny's name was one of the five guys listed, and that Ricky D'Amico's name appeared on the list of girls.

Well, I certainly didn't vote for her.

Everyone listens as Denise Holmes, our class president, reads the results at the microphone on the bandstand.

"Our *queen*," she says, glittering, "is head cheerleader and the chair of the prom committee . . . Ricky D'Amico!"

I don't think anyone is surprised by the selection. Whatever else Ricky is, she is certainly popular. And, as always, she is stunning in her emerald dress as she makes her way out onto the dance floor to receive her crown. She looks expectantly out at the crowd.

"And for our *king*," Denise Holmes says, "I'm sure you'll all be pleased to learn that it's our own king of the basketball court . . . Danny Stanton!"

The basketball players all rise to their feet, shouting, "*Da*-nny! *Da*-nny! *Da*-nny!" as they clap their hands and stomp their feet to the rhythm they are creating with his name.

I turn to Danny as he starts to rise from his chair, a half smile on his face. I'm the only one close enough to him to hear it when he says, "No," the rest of the crowd able only to read his lips over the din.

"What?" Denise Holmes cups her hand over her ear. "I can't hear you."

"No," Danny says much louder, and everyone completely shuts up, the room screeching to a silent halt. "No." He smiles more fully this time. "But thanks." He looks down at me, and it is his widest smile yet. "I'm too busy with . . . other things, to assume any courtly duties."

There are groans around the room.

"Really," Danny says. "Just go to whoever's next on the list."

Whatever happens next, whoever gets crowned king

instead of Danny, I don't even notice. I am too busy staring at him. I am dimly aware of applause in the background, and then the music starts again. It is an old song, Eric Clapton's "Wonderful Tonight."

Danny rises, holds out his hand to me. "Dance with me?" he says.

I start to shake my head, but he says softly, "Come on. I've been waiting for this all night."

He leads me out onto the dance floor, and suddenly I am surrounded by other couples, all crowded together. Even as I feel his arms go around me, I hear, or imagine I can hear, the sound of people whispering around us.

"What is he doing with her?" "Can you believe he turned down being king?" "If it wasn't for her, he'd—"

I look quickly to see if he's bothered by this, but all I see is him smiling down at me, and I can see that, no matter what he does, he will always be Danny Stanton, and nothing will ever touch him.

And I can also see that, okay, maybe I will always be that person in the room that everyone talks about. And maybe that is okay now.

Being in Danny's arms like this, being dressed like this on this night, even if everyone is whispering, it is like I am having the magical evening I hoped for. I know it's silly in a way, silly in the face of the seriousness that lies ahead, and yet I cannot fault myself for wanting what everyone else has for just one night, can't fault myself for being thrilled with the magic of it all.

"You do," Danny says.

"Excuse me?" I say. I'm not following.

"The song," he says. "You do look wonderful tonight."

And then he bends his head to kiss me, his lips touching mine so softly it is like my lips are brushing up against the wings of an angel.

Danny pulls back, just a bit.

"I love you, Angel," he says.

"I—I—I—*ow*!"

"What?" he says, pulling back so he can look at my face more closely. "What's wrong?"

But then that sharp feeling I just experienced subsides, and I move toward him again, smile into his dark eyes.

"It was nothing," I say. "Must have been one of those Braxton Hicks contractions the Lamaze instructor told us about. You know, the false alarms."

Certainly, I am the only girl at the senior prom experiencing false contractions.

Afterward, when everyone else goes off for the after-prom and early breakfast, Danny takes me home. Sure, it would be fun to go too, but I have had my shot at normalcy for the night, and now I am just a very pregnant girl who needs her sleep more than anything else.

Outside my parents' front door, as the limo waits, Danny kisses me one more time, good night. It is a lovely kiss, but when he breaks away, he doesn't repeat what he said earlier in the evening right before I had the false contraction, that he loves me, and I don't say anything about it either. I am sure he must have said it just from the excitement of the moment.

"I'll call you tomorrow," he says, "see how you're doing."

"Okay," I say. And then for once, making the bold move, I go up on tiptoe, kiss him softly on the lips. "Thanks," I say, "for everything."

Inside, my parents are up watching TV as if they are normally up this late watching TV, which they never are.

"How did it go?" my dad says, eyes still on the TV, pretending not to be really interested.

My mother masks her curiosity less well, snatching the remote from his hand and clicking off the screen.

"How did it go?" she asks anxiously.

"It was . . . *wonderful*," I say, melting.

"Really?" She's shocked. "Tell me all about it. Would you like a snack?"

"I could make some eggs," my dad says.

"Tomorrow," I say, floating up the stairs as if on a cloud, or at least I float as well as I can with my bulk. "There'll be time enough tomorrow."

In the bathroom I take the gold stars and glitter out of my hair. In my bedroom I remove my pretty dress, gently hang it over a chair back, put on the oversize pink T-shirt I've taken to wearing to bed. As I pull back the covers, turn out the lights, I relive the evening in my mind, at least the good parts. The clock downstairs starts to chime, and as I lie down, as the old day ticks over into a new one, seven days before I am due to have this baby, my water breaks and I go into labor.

Week of May 27/Week 39

Labor is harder than I ever could have imagined it being.

"Mom! Dad! Come quick!" I'd shouted while still at home. I could almost feel my mind fill with panic and confusion as my body was hit with another contraction, much stronger than the one earlier in the evening. This contraction wasn't joking around.

"What is it, An—," my dad said, rushing in.

"Omigod," my mother said, right behind him, "her water's broken. We've got to get her to the hospital."

"You call the hospital and tell them we're coming in," my dad said. "I'll start the car." Then he scooped me up in his arms as though I weighed only fifty pounds, not a hundred and fifty.

"I can walk, Dad," I said. "I'm not a baby."

"Why take any chances?" he said, carrying me out to the car.

"Call Danny!" I yelled over his shoulder to my mom. "Don't forget to call Danny!"

Danny was already at the hospital when we arrived, despite the look my mother shot me when I yelled for her to call him. He still had his tux on, although the bow tie was undone, and as another contraction hit me, I figured he hadn't been as quick to change as I had.

"You can do this thing," my dad says now.

"You're going to be just fine, honey," my mom says.

We leave them behind in the waiting room as the nurse leads us to the labor room.

"We want room number one," Danny says, remembering the Lamaze instructor's words.

"Room number one's taken," says the nurse, who seems bored. I guess she goes through this every night, but for us it is the one and only.

"Room number two, then," Danny says.

"That's taken too," she says, leading us to an ordinary room. "We've got a full house tonight."

"It's okay," I tell Danny, even as I feel another contraction starting. "I never would've used that Jacuzzi in front of you anyway."

The labor is more painful than I can say, going on for longer than I imagined possible. There are just no words for how awful the pain is. After the night I had sex with Tim O'Mara, I remembered nothing of the act itself: not pain, not pleasure. All I remembered was the sensation of everything slipping away from me and the exact way the stars looked, winking overhead.

There are no stars to look at now, and despite everything the books say about pregnant women later forgetting how painful labor and delivery are, because otherwise there would be a much smaller human race, I know that I will remember every single second of this pain, its length and breadth, as though it were a perfect hard diamond.

But between the bursts of pain, there are glimpses of joy. While my contractions are still ten minutes apart, between them Danny walks me along the hospital corridor, reminding me that the Lamaze instructor said physical activity and remaining upright would help the baby come out more quickly: gravity.

"Maybe you could call the baby Gravity," Danny says, his hand firm under my elbow.

"I don't think so," I say.

"So what will you name her instead?" he asks. I have convinced him the baby is a girl.

"You'll see soon enough," I say.

But soon enough doesn't come soon enough, and the hours of pain, fear too, go on. It is hard to believe, at moments, that it is possible to withstand so much pain and still keep going.

Then things start to move more quickly. But the maternity ward is full tonight—Dr. Caldwell actually has two other patients delivering—and it takes a while for the nurse to bring her.

"Okay," Dr. Caldwell says, snapping on rubber gloves, "let's see what we've got here."

My feet are in the stirrups, sweat beading my face, as she looks between my legs, sees what's there to see.

"Oh, my," she says. "What I'm seeing here is that we've got a baby coming." She looks up at me. "Now's your big moment, Angel. I'm going to need you to push."

Half of my mind screams, *Can I do this? How can I do this?*

Then one of Danny's arms is around my back supporting me upward as he holds tight to my hand with his other hand, and I squeeze back, not even caring if I hurt him. I hold on to that hand tighter than I have ever held on to anything.

"I love you, Angel," he says.

"I love you, Danny," I say back, finally.

"Now . . . *push!*" he says.

And I do what I could not have imagined doing a moment before: I hold on to his hand tighter still as, with eyes wide open, I push my baby out and into the world.

june

I WISH I COULD SAY THAT EVERYTHING WILL TURN OUT ALL right, but I do not know the future yet, do I? And, anyway, life is not an *ABC Afterschool Special*. Not that there's anything wrong with *ABC Afterschool Special*s — life just isn't like that.

I do not know what is around the next corner.

Karin will undoubtedly go off to Yale. Hopefully we will still stay in touch. Hopefully we will remain best friends. But I know that, going on different paths as we have, it will take work to achieve that.

Danny will undoubtedly do well at UConn, at least at basketball. I know that, for a while, he will still want to be a part of *this*, here with me. But who knows how long that can last, will last?

I don't delude myself into believing that there is going to be some neat little happily-ever-after for me. I don't delude myself into thinking that any of this is going to be easy. If life is not an *ABC Afterschool Special*, it is also not a fairy tale, even though some moments may make it seem so.

My story should come with a warning, and that warning should say, in big letters, "HEY, KIDS, DON'T TRY THIS AT HOME!"

I will go to the community college, in three months, as planned. My mom will help take care of the baby during the days. But I don't know if I will ever see my other dream come true, my dream of being a writer.

I don't know if I will ever go on a proper date again, if I will ever feel as though I am like other people again.

I do know that I probably would not have chosen this if I were poor, would not have felt free to choose this if I were poor, if I didn't have so many people behind me.

I do know that my parents didn't have to help me, Danny didn't have to help me—these are the choices *they* made, although I know that, in the future, they may make different choices.

And then I think that all I do know now, as I sit alone on my parents' porch on this hot early day in June, as

I gaze down at Jo asleep in my arms, is that she is the most beautiful thing I have seen in my life.

And, in this moment, that has to be enough.

And, for today, it is.